Laura breathed in the scent of leather and cologne and man as the rain teemed around them, enclosing them in a private world under the umbrella.

She had expected to walk back to her hotel the way she'd come, via the floodlit Piazza San Marco, but Domenico took her back along silent, dimly lit alleys punctuated by bridges. Domenico paused on a bridge to point out the moon's reflection on the water.

His arm tightened and she held up her face as he bent his head to kiss her. Their lips met in a gentle exploratory caress that quickly flared into something so different that in some corner of her brain Laura marveled at Domenico's skill in keeping the umbrella upright. As he kissed her with a mounting passion, she responded helplessly, her hands tunneling under his jacket to hold him closer. At last he gave a smothered groan and raised his head a fraction, his breath hot against her cheek as he held her hard against him.

"Now you see?" he said, in a voice husky with emotion.

"Yes," she whispered shakily.

CATHERINE GEORGE was born in Wales, and early on developed a passion for reading which eventually fuelled her compulsion to write. Marriage to an engineer led to nine years in Brazil, but on his later travels the education of her son and daughter kept her in the U.K. And instead of constant reading to pass her lonely evenings, she began to write the first of her romantic novels. When not writing and reading she loves to cook, listen to opera and browse in antique shops.

Catherine George

A VENETIAN PASSION

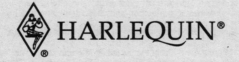

TORONTO • NEW YORK • LONDON
AMSTERDAM • PARIS • SYDNEY • HAMBURG
STOCKHOLM • ATHENS • TOKYO • MILAN • MADRID
PRAGUE • WARSAW • BUDAPEST • AUCKLAND

ISBN 0-373-18858-7

A VENETIAN PASSION

First North American Publication 2005.

www.eHarlequin.com

Printed in U.S.A.

CHAPTER ONE

THE flight from Heathrow was punctual. For this at least he was thankful. His eyes smouldered. If any other man—or woman—had asked him to meet the plane in person he would have refused. With impatience he scanned the new arrivals streaming through the Marco Polo concourse. Many of them were young women with fair hair, but none seemed to be travelling alone. At last he saw a solitary female figure hurrying in his direction, dragging a small suitcase on wheels. His eyes narrowed. It could be. A white cotton sunhat was pulled low over a face hidden by enormous sunglasses, but she was young, small, and the rope of hair hanging down her back was most definitely blonde.

'Miss Green?' he said, moving to intercept her.

She turned warily. 'Yes?'

'Welcome to Venice.' He bowed slightly. 'I am Domenico Chiesa, from the Forli Group. Signor Lorenzo Forli, the *Presidente*, asked me to meet you.'

She smiled in surprise. 'Really? How very kind of him.'

It is even kinder of me, he thought irritably. 'Come. You need a ticket for the *vaporetto*.' He hurried her to the office near the exit. 'The No.1 Aligaluna waterbus leaves almost at once.' He bought a ticket and handed it over with a diagram showing the route from the Piazza San Marco to her hotel. 'This will help you find the Locanda Verona, Miss Green.'

She smiled politely as she accepted it. 'Thank you. Goodbye.'

'I regret—' he began, but she was already hurrying away to the quayside. He stared after her, lips compressed. He had been about to say he was too busy to make the journey with

5

her, but the lady, it seemed, had not expected—or desired—
him to do that. His eyes darkened as he boarded a water taxi.
He had been forced to leave a very difficult situation to come
to Marco Polo, but he had dutifully guided the lady to the
right *vaporetto* and given her directions to the hotel he had
personally arranged for her. Yet her gratitude had been all
for Lorenzo Forli, who had merely given orders from group
headquarters in Florence. Here in Venice Miss Laura Green
had virtually ignored the man who had taken time he could
not spare to meet her.

Unaware that she'd given offence, Laura managed to find
a space at the rail of the *vaporetto* to get the best view, deeply
grateful to Lorenzo Forli for arranging her trip to Venice.
She knew from the guidebook that this particular boat travelled down the Grand Canal slowly enough for passengers to
gaze at the architecture, and she settled down to enjoy every
second of the journey as each ancient, fragile building and
palazzo succeeded another, some seeming almost to lean together for support. Amazing! It was her first visit to Venice,
yet everything seemed so extraordinarily familiar, as though
she'd been here before. The media was responsible for the
déjà vu feeling, of course. Venice was the most filmed and
photographed city on the planet.

Laura's excitement mounted as she saw the famous bell
tower soaring high above Piazza San Marco, and when the
boat docked she was among the first of the stream of passengers to pass the lion of St Mark high on his pillar. As she
reached the *piazza* she gazed in awe at the oriental extravagance of the Basilica as she threaded through the crowds
clustered at its central entrance, and looked with longing
down its great length. She couldn't wait to explore this fabulous square, but right now the first priority was to find the
Locanda Verona. Her Italian lessons at school had never actually been put into practice, so even if she managed to ask
directions there would be no earthly chance of understanding

a reply. Laura checked with the diagram, settled her canvas satchel across her chest, and trundled her suitcase through the tourists and pigeons to cross the vast, arcaded *piazza*. To her delight the pair of bronze Moors on the clock tower struck the hour as she neared the arch below them, and she stopped to watch before passing through on her way to the famous Mercerie, where she'd read that shops tempted visitors all the way to the Rialto. But not this visitor right now, she thought with regret. According to the brusque Mr Chiesa's diagram her hotel was situated somewhere beyond in the network of narrow streets called *calles*, where the canals were spanned by the famous bridges of Venice. And eventually, after only a couple of wrong turnings, Laura found a bridge that led her right to the door of the hotel.

The Locanda Verona was a small guest house with ochre-coloured walls and typical Venetian windows, and, most important of all to Laura, surprisingly affordable charges for the San Marco area. The high-ceilinged reception hall was blessedly cool after the late afternoon heat and the smile of the handsome woman at the desk reassuringly friendly as she introduced herself in careful English as Maddalena Rossi, wife of the owner. Once the usual formalities were over she conducted Laura to a room on the top floor.

'The room is small, but you have your own bathroom, Miss Green,' Signora Rossi announced, unlocking the door. 'I hope you will be comfortable here.'

'I can't fail to be!' Laura gazed in delight at the vaulted, wood-beamed ceiling and the Botticelli print over the pristine white of the bed.

Signora Rossi moved past the bed to a pair of narrow, half-glazed doors and with a flourish opened them onto a small roof garden. 'Here is your view.'

Laura took in a deep breath as she looked down on the picturesque buildings lining the canal below. 'And what a wonderful view it is! Thank you very much indeed.'

Looking pleased, the *signora* reminded Laura that meals were not provided. 'But there are many eating places close by. Information on these can be obtained at the reception desk.'

After a call home to her mother to report safe arrival, Laura unpacked, took a swift shower, then got to work with a hot brush until her hair was dry enough to coil up in a smooth twist. She made up her face with the speed of long practice, put on a plain black dress packed as a safe choice for eating out alone in Venice, and went downstairs to tell Signora Rossi where she was going as she left her key at the desk. At last, her eyes gleaming with anticipation, Laura went out into the warm evening and crossed the bridge over the canal to find her way back through the picturesque alleys to the Piazza San Marco. Her goal was the famous Café Florian, where she knew one could sit at a table and listen to the house orchestra, all for the price of coffee or wine. But for her first night only Laura meant to lash out on a snack of some kind as well, whatever it cost, to celebrate her arrival in Venice.

A waiter led her to a table in the open air at exactly the right distance from the orchestra in its bower of greenery, and in the careful, schoolgirl Italian she'd been practising all the way to the *piazza* Laura asked for mineral water and a cheese and ham sandwich. Maybe she'd go wild and have coffee later, but right now she was content just to sit here in the floodlit magnificence of the square and listen to the hum of multi-lingual conversation blending with the music. When the waiter brought her order she made her *tramezzino* last as long as possible while she watched the passing show of people enjoying a leisurely evening stroll through the great square. Some were couples, others entire groups who stopped to talk with friends, with much kissing of cheeks and children part of the scene. Laura gazed at it all with intense pleasure, so absorbed that at first the sound of her own name failed to register.

'Miss Green?' repeated a deep, husky voice. *'Buona sera.'*

Laura turned sharply to see Domenico Chiesa looking down at her, an arrested look on his face.

She smiled, surprised. 'Good evening.'

He returned the smile with warmth and charm very different from the impatience that had radiated from him at the airport. 'I called first at the Locanda Verona. Signora Rossi told me you would be here. I trust that everything is to your satisfaction at the hotel?'

Laura assured him that it was. And now she had attention to spare for Domenico Chiesa found he was worth looking at. Shoulders broad, hips slim, waving dark hair cut as perfectly as the superb suit he wore. And without the dark glasses his oval, heavy-lidded eyes were a striking aquamarine blue with a look in them that told her he was well aware of every last one of his physical assets.

'I was so intent on the passing show in the *piazza* I didn't see you arrive,' she told him.

'And I startled you. To make amends may I offer you wine, or coffee?'

Laura hesitated for a moment, then thought, Why not? 'Thank you. I'd like a *caffè macchiato*, please.'

'Your accent is most charming,' he told her, and raised a slim hand. He gave the order to the waiter, then indicated the chair next to Laura's and said, *'Permesso?'*

'Of course.' What else could she say? Besides, no woman in her right mind would turn down attractive male company in surroundings like these, with a moon overhead and music playing.

'So, Miss Green,' he said, after their coffee arrived, 'what is your first impression of my city?'

Laura looked round her at the glittering, extravagantly beautiful Piazza San Marco. 'I've seen it countless times in films and television programmes, but Venice for real is breathtaking.'

'I am glad it pleases you.'

'I would be very hard to please if it didn't!' She sipped her coffee with relish. 'A friend told me to make Florian's my first call, Signor Chiesa.'

'A wise choice.' He smiled at her. 'But, please, my name is Domenico.'

'As you know, I'm Laura,' she said, returning the smile.

'So, Laura, what are your plans for tomorrow?'

'Just to wander round your amazing city.' She put down her empty cup.

'You wish for more coffee?' he said at once.

She shook her head. 'It was delicious, but no more, thank you.'

He smiled persuasively. 'Join me in a glass of Prosecco instead.'

Once again there was no way to refuse. Besides, Laura reminded herself, he was probably just acting on instructions. Fen had said that Lorenzo would order some underling to make the holiday arrangements—though anyone less like an underling than Domenico Chiesa was hard to imagine.

'*Salute!*' he said, raising his glass to her once the Prosecco had arrived. 'Do you know Signor Forli well?'

'I've just met him at my friend's house a couple of times. He's married to her sister.' She drank some of her wine. 'Do you live here in Venice?'

He nodded. 'All my life. Where is your home?'

'My family's home is in the country in Gloucestershire, but I work and live in London.'

'And what do you do there, Laura?' he asked, and listened with flattering attention as she gave a brief description of her work as researcher at a Docklands investment bank.

'I am impressed,' he told her, then with a sigh of regret finished his wine and rose to his feet. 'Now I must return to my own duties. But first allow me to escort you back to the Locanda Verona.'

Laura shook her head, smiling. She'd said yes to him quite enough. 'That's very kind of you, but I think I'll stay on and listen to the orchestra a little longer. Thank you for the drinks, Signor—'

'Domenico, *per favore*!' He smiled down into her eyes. '*Buona sera*, Laura.'

'Goodnight.'

Laura watched him walk away, amused by the touch—more than a touch—of arrogance in his bearing. She'd noticed it in all the native male population she'd seen so far, including the waiters. It was obviously a man thing, Venetian style. She watched him until he was out of sight, and after a while, no longer enjoying the evening quite so much now she was alone, looked round for her missing bill. She bent to look under the table, then signalled to a waiter.

'*Il conto, per favore?*'

'*Scusa?*' he said, puzzled.

Oh, boy, thought Laura. 'Do you speak English?' she asked hopefully.

'A little,' he said with caution.

'I've lost my bill, and I want to pay.'

'Ah!' His face cleared. 'It is paid, *signorina*.'

Her eyebrows rose. 'All of it?'

'Yes, *signorina*.'

Surprised, Laura gave him a tip, wished him goodnight and strolled slowly back to the Locanda Verona.

Laura woke early next morning, stared blankly for a moment at the wood-beamed ceiling, then grinned like the Cheshire cat. She was in Venice! She got out of bed and stood at the glass doors, stretching luxuriously as she gazed at the view. First on the agenda was breakfast. She hadn't eaten much in the way of dinner last night. And what she had eaten Domenico had paid for, she thought guiltily. But whatever he did at his hotel he obviously earned a good salary by the way he dressed. Besides, she probably came under the heading of expenses claimed from Lorenzo Forli.

In jeans and white T-shirt, her hair in a loose braid down her back, Laura went downstairs to ask about the nearest source of breakfast. Armed with directions from Signora Rossi, she found the small bar recommended and ordered coffee and an almond croissant to enjoy while she consulted her guidebook. Some intensive window-shopping was first on the agenda before she actually bought any presents to take home. She finished her coffee, put on dark glasses and sunhat and went off to spend time gazing in jewellers' windows in the arcades of the Piazza San Marco before salivating over the gorgeous clothes in the stylish shops just off it. Later, remembering to keep to the right among the crush of fellow tourists, she set out on an immensely enjoyable tour of the famous Mercerie, and did her best to look in every shop and boutique all the way to the Rialto. When she reached the famous bridge at last she wandered, fascinated, round the colourful food markets for a while before stopping at a small bar nearby. She ordered mineral water and a roll stuffed with roast ham, and ate standing up again, because her guidebook said it was cheaper than sitting at a table. But after lunch her feet began to complain, and Laura lost her zest for window-shopping. The walk to the Locanda Verona in the afternoon heat seemed so much longer on the way back that her first priority when she got to her room was a long, cool shower followed by a read on her bed, with her hair spread out on a towel over her shoulders to dry.

The read turned into a siesta and when Laura woke the afternoon was gone. She slid out of bed in a rush, annoyed at wasting so much time in it, and stooped to pick up an envelope that someone had pushed under her door while she was sleeping. Her eyebrows shot to her hair as she read the brief note inside. Domenico Chiesa requested the pleasure of her company at dinner that evening and would call for her at eight. And he was so sure she'd be delighted with the idea there was no address or contact number on the note for her reply. She whistled inelegantly. He'd changed his tune a bit since their first encounter! He'd hustled her off to the boat at the airport as though he couldn't get rid of her fast enough. Yet he'd turned up at Florian's later, apparently just to make sure all was well with her—Lorenzo's idea, probably. She shrugged. She was on such a tight budget that dinner with a handsome Venetian was an offer she'd be mad to refuse. But delightful though her small room might be she had no intention of staying put in it until he called for her.

Laura spent more time than usual on her face, then, mindful of Fen's advice to dress to kill if she went somewhere special, put on the second of her three dresses, a silky sheath the colour of ripe raspberries. She piled her hair up in an artfully precarious knot that took ages to get right, clipped on gold filigree earrings and went downstairs to leave a message for Domenico Chiesa at the reception desk.

Laura strolled out into the warm evening with a smile on her face as she pictured the self-assured Domenico's reaction when he found the bird had flown. Not that she was flying far—just to Florian's again to watch the world go by until he came to find her. If he came at all. If his original attitude was anything to go by his male Venetian pride might well be offended because she hadn't stayed put to wait for him. Though why he'd made the invitation in the first place was a mystery. Lorenzo's instructions to look after her could hardly have gone that far.

Domenico Chiesa could have told her precisely why as he made for the Locanda Verona later. At the airport Miss Laura Green had been so eager to board the *vaporetto* she had paid no attention to him at all. Such treatment from a woman was new to him, and instead of amusing him, as it would have done any other time, her indifference had irritated him. But later that evening he'd had a drink with a friend in the San Marco area, and on impulse called at the Locanda Verona afterwards to check that all was well with the girl—and to make a better impression, he admitted, laughing at himself. But when he'd eventually found her it had taken much control to hide his surprise.

At Marco Polo her face had been hidden by the hat and glasses. But at Florian's he'd discovered that her mouth curved delightfully as she smiled, and the dark amber shade of her eyes was unexpected below the shining coil of flaxen hair. Her face had too much character for mere beauty, possibly, but she possessed that indefinable something he found so desirable in a woman he had automatically set out to charm. Then she had given him the second surprise of the evening by refusing his escort to her hotel—another first in his experience. The cool Miss Laura Green was most definitely a challenge. Domenico's eyes gleamed with anticipation. As first step in the warming-up process he would impress her by taking her to Harry's Bar, the Mecca of all foreign visitors. Then later, when she was mellow with good food and wine, he would provide the finishing touch to the evening with a moonlit ride in a gondola.

Domenico strode into the modest little hotel like Caesar bent on conquering Gaul. Then stared in disbelief when he heard that the young lady had gone out.

'*Cosa?*'

Signora Rossi smiled apologetically and handed him a note.

Domenico thanked her, read the brief missive, and after bidding the *signora* good evening strode outside again, eyes stormy, strongly tempted to leave Miss Laura Green sitting alone at Florian's all evening. But his irritation vanished when he found her in the *piazza*. She sat, composed, watching the evening parade, the vibrant colour of her dress the perfect foil for her gleaming hair. Tonight she had knotted this up in a sexy, insecure arrangement that looked as though one touch of a lover's hand would bring it tumbling down. Escaping tendrils lay on her neck in the exact place that invited the touch of a man's lips, and to Domenico's surprise he found he strongly objected to the admiring male glances she was attracting as she sipped from a long glass.

Unknown to him Laura had spotted Domenico the moment he appeared in the *piazza*. She'd monitored his progress from the corner of her eye, admiring the perfection of his pale linen suit and beautiful shoes. But she waited until he reached her table before looking up with a cool little smile to say hello.

'*Buona sera.*' He returned the smile reproachfully. 'You did not wait for me.'

She shrugged in apology. 'I left a message for you with Signora Rossi. My stay in Venice is too short to waste it in my room.'

'Your room is not satisfactory?' he demanded.

'Quite the reverse; it's charming. But when your note arrived I'd already spent the entire afternoon there. In bed.' Laura smiled into the spectacular blue eyes. 'After a morning of relentless window-shopping I slept far longer than I intended.'

He took the chair beside her. 'You will drink Prosecco, yes?'

The man took a lot for granted! Laura eyed him in amusement as he gave the order. Domenico Chiesa was too sure of himself by half.

'So, Laura,' he said, turning back to her. 'You looked in shop windows. Did you buy anything?'

'Not today. My plan was to look first and buy later, but I saw so many things I lusted after I can't remember where I saw what. If you see what I mean,' she said, smiling.

'You do not think my English sufficient to understand?' he demanded.

'I think your English is wonderful,' she said hastily. 'I just wish I could speak Italian a fraction as well.'

The blue eyes gleamed. 'I could teach you.'

I bet you could, thought Laura, and not just syntax, either. She smiled regretfully. 'I'm not staying long enough for that.'

The waiter arrived with the wine, and Domenico sat back in his chair, contemplating her over the rim of his glass in silence for a moment or two. 'Tell me, Laura Green,' he said at last, 'is there someone in London waiting with impatience for your return?'

'You mean a man?'

'*Naturalmente.*' He looked at her small, capable left hand. 'I see no ring, but you must have a lover. How could you not?' he added matter-of-factly.

She looked him in the eye. 'Are you always this direct with someone you've just met?'

'No,' he said, and smiled disarmingly. 'But you interest me, Laura. If you do not wish to answer, I understand,' he added.

She hesitated, reluctant to discuss something so personal. But after skipping off earlier instead of waiting for Domenico it seemed best not to offend again. 'There's no one right now,' she said at last. 'There was someone until quite recently, a doctor in the training stage in a hospital, but not a lover the way you mean.'

'Ah!' He nodded, satisfied. 'You did not love him with passion.'

The outrageously personal statement was so accurate Laura nodded wryly. 'Romance just isn't my thing. I'm the strictly practical type.'

'You will meet someone one day who will change all that,' he assured her, and got to his feet. 'Come. It is time to eat.'

Laura felt a pang of remorse as he paid for the wine. 'Domenico, I do apologise. I haven't thanked you yet for paying my bill last night. You shouldn't have done that, but it was very kind of you.'

'It was my pleasure,' he said casually, and glanced down at her feet. 'You can walk in those delightful shoes?'

'How far?'

'Only to Harry's Bar. It is quite near.'

'No problem, then,' she said, impressed. Her holiday budget wouldn't stretch to meals in such exalted places.

Domenico Chiesa did not, it was obvious, suffer from the same problem. When he ushered Laura through a surprisingly unimpressive door and took her upstairs, the head waiter in Harry's Bar greeted him by name. The dining room was plain by Venetian standards, with half-panelled walls and large black and white photographs of American landmarks, but it was full except for the table reserved for Signor Chiesa.

'The restaurant is a little austere, and there is no terrace, but it never lacks for patrons,' Domenico told her.

'I can see that,' said Laura, eyeing the crowded room. 'I know that Hemingway and Churchill used to come here, but are there any celebrities around tonight?'

'None that I know,' he said dismissively.

Her eyes danced. 'You mean that if Domenico Chiesa doesn't know them they're not celebrities?'

'You are mocking me,' he accused, laughing. 'And now,' he added as a waiter set glasses in front of them, 'you must taste the cocktail first created here.'

'A Bellini?' said Laura, eyeing the drink with respect.

Domenico raised his glass. 'Enjoy.'

Enjoy was the right word, she thought as she tasted the famous mix of fresh white peach juice and sparkling Prosecco. 'Mmm, fabulous!'

'*Bene!*' he said with satisfaction. 'Now, tell me what you like to eat.'

Choosing their meal was a serious business. When Laura firmly refused a first course Domenico described the main dishes in detail, teasing her because she wasn't brave enough to try *carpaccio*, the raw, marinated beef of his own choice. Eventually, after much discussion, she settled for pasta baked with *prosciutto*, and enjoyed it enormously, but shook her head regretfully when Domenico suggested the house speciality of rich chocolate cake for dessert afterwards.

'Thank you, but I couldn't eat another thing.'

'Then we shall drink coffee while you tell me your plans for tomorrow.'

'I thought I'd go shopping for presents before I make a start on the local culture. I want something special for my mother, my sister, and my closest friend,' she said, ticking off her fingers, 'and inexpensive things—if there are such things in Venice—for friends at the bank.' She smiled at him. 'Any advice for the tourist would be welcome.'

Domenico gazed at her thoughtfully for a moment, then smiled back. 'I can do more than that. Tomorrow I shall show you the best places to find your souvenirs of Venezia.'

Laura looked at him in silence for so long he raised an eyebrow in silent question.

'Domenico,' she said at last, 'why are you doing this?'

'This?' he repeated innocently.

She nodded. 'I can't believe that Lorenzo Forli asked you to go to such lengths to look after me!'

'This is true,' he admitted. 'He asked me to arrange a hotel, meet you at the airport and escort you to the *vaporetto*, and afterwards check to see that you were happy with your hotel.' The spectacular eyes locked with hers. 'I did as he wanted. But now, Laura, I am doing what *I* want.'

She held the gaze steadily. 'In that case I need to ask you the question you asked me.'

'And what is that?'

'Is there someone in *your* life?'

'No.' He shrugged an expressive shoulder. 'There was. Now there is not.'

'Snap,' she said, sighing.

'Snap? What is this?'

'It means the same thing. I recently had someone in my life, too, but not any more.'

Domenico's eyes softened. 'This makes you sad, Laura?'

She shook her head. 'Relieved, not sad. I'd known Edward for years, but not as well as I thought. I had no idea he was into embarrassing romantic gestures.'

There was a pause while coffee was served.

'I am very curious,' said Domenico, leaning nearer when they were alone. 'What did this romantic man do?'

'He took me out to dinner one night. But when the waiter took the lid off a serving dish there was a diamond ring sitting there instead of the salmon I'd asked for.' Laura shuddered. 'And right there in front of all the other diners Edward went down on one knee and asked me to marry him.'

'*Dio!* What did you do?'

'There was no way I could possibly humiliate him in public so I let him put the ring on my finger and kiss me, and everyone applauded.' She smiled crookedly. 'When I handed the ring back in the taxi afterwards Edward rejected my offer of friendship pretty violently. So we don't see each other any more.'

'This does not surprise me. When a man is in love it is not friendship he desires from his woman.' Domenico got up suddenly. '*Mi scusi*, Laura, I must leave you for a moment.'

Laura watched him cross the room to speak to a waiter, who nodded quickly, pocketed the money he was given, and left the dining room. When Domenico rejoined her he pressed her to more coffee, but she shook her head.

'Nothing else, thank you. It was such a wonderful meal. Thank you for bringing me here.'

'Thank *you* for the pleasure of your company.'

Laura had expected to walk back to her hotel the way she came, via the floodlit Piazza San Marco, but Domenico took her back along silent, dimly lit alleys punctuated by bridges. He pointed out landmarks and gave her the names of the different *calles* as they strolled, and eventually, when they were on territory that was beginning to feel familiar, he paused on a bridge to point out the moon's reflection in the water.

'By day it is best not to linger on our bridges, but at night when it is quiet we may do so for a moment. In the past there were no railings,' he informed her. 'This meant taking much care at night.'

She gave a sudden chuckle, and he took her hand and looked down into her face.

'What amuses you, Laura?'

'I was just thinking that to a practical soul like me your city is too romantic for words, Domenico.'

'Ah, but Venezia is not always kind to us as she is tonight,' he assured her. 'We have fog and rain and floods in winter.'

'I can't imagine it right now.'

'Then you must come back again to Venice and see for yourself,' he said, and drew her nearer.

'I must get back to the hotel right now,' she said hastily.

'Let us say goodnight here first.' He took her gently by the shoulders and kissed her on both cheeks, looked down into her eyes for a moment, then bent his head to capture her mouth in a kiss of unexpected tenderness.

'I was told that I'd have no problem with the average Italian male,' she said breathlessly when he raised his head. Not that there was anything average about Domenico Chiesa.

He smiled and took her hand to resume walking. 'One kiss is a problem?'

'I suppose not.'

'It will be a problem for me if you now refuse my assistance with your shopping.'

'I won't.' Laura grinned at him and he laughed, his hand tightening on hers. 'Find me bargains and I forget the kiss.'

'But I shall not,' he said, with such a theatrical sigh she laughed at him.

'You expect me to believe that?'

'It is the truth,' he assured her. 'I shall lie awake all night thinking of the touch of your lips against mine.'

She chuckled. 'And where will you spend this sleepless night? At the hotel you work in?'

He shook his head. 'I have a small apartment right here in San Marco. Tonight I shall sleep—or not sleep—only a short distance away from you, Miss Laura Green.' He smiled down at her and raised her hand to his lips. 'I have enjoyed this evening very much. I shall call for you at nine tomorrow and we shall eat breakfast together. Sleep well.'

CHAPTER TWO

LAURA found it hard to sleep at all for a while. The long afternoon nap was partly to blame, but Domenico's kiss had rather more to do with it. She frowned in the darkness. If this was the effect Venice was having on her it was a good thing she wasn't staying long.

After her restless night Laura woke late next morning and rushed through a shower, slapped on moisturiser and lipstick, wove her hair into a loose braid, pulled on a mint-green T-shirt and white cotton trousers and raced down to the reception hall to find Domenico, in jeans with a shirt that matched his eyes, talking to Signora Rossi.

'*Buon giorno*, Laura,' he said, smiling, and took away what breath she had left by kissing her on both cheeks. 'Did you sleep well?'

'Like a baby,' she lied.

'Then let us begin.'

During breakfast, which she enjoyed all the more for sitting down to eat it, Laura told Domenico what she had in mind.

'I've been reading up about shopping in my guidebook, so I've made a list. First priority is a pair of the velvet slippers worn here for Carnival for my mother.'

'And for your father?'

Her eyes fell. 'My father's dead.'

'*Mi dispiace!*' said Domenico swiftly, and laid his hand on hers.

'You didn't know. Now,' she added briskly, 'where do we start?'

Shopping with Domenico Chiesa was a very pleasant experience. He took Laura to places she would have had no hope of finding on her own, and seemed to enjoy it all as much as she did. He hunted down an authentic gold carnival mask, helped Laura choose pretty, inexpensive Venetian glass earrings and T-shirts in vivid colours printed with the Venezia logo, and at last took her to the stalls at the foot of the Ponte delle Guglie on Strada Nuova for crimson velvet slippers for her mother.

'And now,' said Domenico firmly, just when Laura felt ready to drop rather than shop any more, 'we must eat.'

She gave him a pleading look. 'Domenico, *please* let me pay for lunch.'

He smiled and shook his head. 'It is already arranged. And you are tired so we shall go by water taxi.'

A journey in a sleek white motorboat was such a different experience from one by *vaporetto* the journey was over far too soon for Laura.

'Thank you, that was fun,' she said as Domenico helped her off the boat. 'But I know it was also expensive so I hope we're eating in a cheaper place than Harry's Bar.'

'I can assure you that we are. With your permission I shall give you lunch in my private retreat.'

Domenico's retreat was an apartment in a converted *palazzo*, with a view of the Grand Canal and the Santa Maria della Salute church. When he ushered her into a compact sitting room with tall windows and apricot walls Laura felt a stab of envy as she took in the gleaming wood floors and white-covered sofas, the shelves with books and the mirrors everywhere.

'This is just lovely.'

'I am glad you like it.' He laid her shopping bags on one of the sofas. 'I thought you might prefer a quiet meal here in peace after your shopping.'

Domenico's dining room was small, but opened onto a balcony with a view of the Grand Canal. He set a meal on the table with speed and efficiency, which impressed Laura as she sat down to Fontina cheese and San Daniele ham served with ripe red tomatoes and salad leaves.

'This is perfect. Exactly what I need. Shopping is tiring, even here in Venice.' She smiled at him gratefully as she buttered a roll. 'I'm so grateful for your help, Domenico. You took me to places I wouldn't have found on my own.' And because of it she had spent far less money than expected.

'I was happy to help,' he assured her. 'Would you like wine?'

'Water, please. If I drink wine at this hour I'll need another sleep, and it's a sin to waste too much time in Venice in bed!'

'Alone, certainly,' he agreed, and laughed at her look. 'Laura, *per favore*! Is that one small, sweet kiss to blame for such dark suspicion? I intend you no harm, I swear.'

'Oh, I know that!' She wagged a finger at him. 'If you did the boss wouldn't like it.'

He looked blank. 'The boss?'

'Lorenzo Forli!'

'Ah, yes.' He got up to take her plate. 'Now, then, Miss Laura Green, I shall make coffee while you rest in the *salotto*.'

'I could help wash the dishes,' she offered, but he shook his head.

'My machine will do that. I shall not be long.'

Laura was standing at one of the tall windows, looking down on the busy waterway, when Domenico came in with a tray. She turned to him with a smile. 'What a priceless view!'

'I am often told I would make much money if I rented my apartment to visitors.'

'You don't like the idea?'

He shook his head as he poured coffee. 'I am constantly surrounded by people at the hotel, therefore I have much need of my private retreat when time allows. Which is not often enough, alas.'

Laura sat down and took the cup he offered her. 'Domenico?'

'*Sì?*'

'Tell me to mind my own business, if you like, but I can't help feeling curious. When we were discussing my love life—or lack of it—you kept pretty quiet about your own.'

'Because it is embarrassing.' He shrugged, and sat down beside her. 'It is no secret. I was engaged to be married while still young, but my *fidanzata* changed her mind.'

'How did you feel about that?'

'Angry.'

Laura looked at him curiously. 'Only angry?'

His face hardened. 'A week before our wedding day Alessa ran away with my oldest friend.'

'Oh, bad luck,' she said with sympathy, and to her relief Domenico let out a crow of laughter.

'That is so British!' He shook his head. 'My *fidanzata* deserts me for another man and all you can say is bad luck?'

'What would you like me to say?'

'You say, "Domenico, my heart bleeds for you",' he said promptly. 'Then you comfort me with many kisses.'

'Oh, right—that's going to happen!'

He smiled at her soulfully. 'I wish so much that it would!'

'When was this, by the way?'

'Ten years ago.'

'Then your heart can't still be bleeding! Have you seen the lady since?'

'Many times. Since her marriage Alessa has gained three children and several kilos in weight.' Domenico gave her a wicked grin. 'And I have received a little comfort from other ladies over the years to assuage my sorrow.'

'I bet! Anyway, I thought you were angry, not sorrowful.'

He was suddenly serious. 'Mario was my friend. He should

have faced me with the truth instead of running away with Alessa like a criminal.'

'Probably they both felt like criminals for hurting you.'

He shrugged. 'Those hurt most were Alessa's parents. They wanted the marriage very much.'

'Because you were a good catch for their daughter?'

'They know my family,' he said simply, as though that explained it. 'Alessa comes from a long line of aristocrats with very little money, and she has two younger sisters. As soon as Alessa left school she was pushed into marriage with someone suitable able to provide for her.'

'Did you know she was being pushed?'

His mouth twisted. 'Of course not. In my arrogance I believed she was madly in love with me. She was very sweet, very pretty. Not long after our first meeting we became engaged, and her parents arranged the wedding.'

'Couldn't they have gone through with it with a different bridegroom?' asked Laura.

Domenico looked amused. 'A practical idea, but not possible. Alessa and Mario were already married by the time they returned to Venice. Their first son was born seven months later,' he added, shrugging.

'Ah. But in that case surely you must have wondered if the child—' She stopped dead. 'Sorry! Forget I said that.'

His lashes came down like shutters. 'The child could not have been mine. Alessa had insisted that we must be married before we made love.'

Laura's eyes widened. 'And you went along with that?'

He shrugged. 'She was so young and shy and—I believed—inexperienced, that I respected her wish.'

'Yet all the time she was sleeping with your best friend. No wonder you were angry.' She eyed him curiously. 'But this was a long time ago. And there must have been other women in your life since then.'

'Of course. I am wary of marriage, not women.' He waved

a hand at the room. 'I have this apartment, I enjoy my work, I travel, and in winter I indulge my passion for skiing. My life suits me very well.'

'So does mine now,' she told him. 'Since the fiasco with Edward I'm keeping men out of my social life for a while. I get quite enough of them during the day. Part of my job involves collating reports to pass on to the likely lads on the trading floor at the bank, and to a man they believe they're irresistible to women!'

Domenico smiled. 'But not to you?'

'Not in the slightest.'

'You dislike them all?'

Laura shook her head. 'Actually, I like some of them well enough. But if I said yes to so much as sharing a pizza with any one of them I'd be asking for trouble.'

He frowned. 'You mean they would also expect to share your bed?'

'From the way they talk, yes. So I say no. Behind my back,' she added tartly, 'they call me the Ice Maiden.'

Domenico nodded sagely. 'And all of them burn to melt the ice!'

She gave a scornful sniff. 'No chance of that.'

'The proposal in the restaurant—this was recent?'

'Very recent. I should have been on holiday in Tuscany with Edward this week, in a villa with some of his college friends and their partners. He sent my share of the cost back to me the day after the quarrel, so because I'd already arranged the time off my mother asked Fen to sort something out for me in Venice. If you work for the Forlis,' she added, 'maybe you know her. Lorenzo Forli is married to her sister Jess.'

'I have met Fenella, yes,' said Domenico. 'What time shall we meet this evening, Laura?'

She looked at him steadily. 'Are we doing something this evening?'

'Yes,' he said firmly. 'I shall take you to a favourite restaurant of mine.'

Secretly delighted with the idea, Laura gave him a militant look. 'I'd like that very much, but on one condition.'

'That I do not kiss you,' he said, resigned.

'That I pay for the meal!'

Domenico held up his hands in laughing surrender, and gave her his phone number. 'Now give me yours.' And although Laura assured him she could find her way back alone, he insisted on walking back with her to the Locanda Verona. 'Sleep for a while,' he advised. 'I shall call for you at seven-thirty.' He speared her with a look of glittering blue command as he left her at the familiar bridge. 'And this time I insist that you wait for me!'

Laura turned suddenly when she was halfway across. 'Domenico! I forgot my shopping.'

He smiled indulgently. '*Non importa.* I shall bring it this evening. *Ciao!*'

Laura smiled her thanks and went into the hotel, her spirits high at the prospect of another evening with Domenico—her third in his company if she added the brief encounter at Florian's. Her eyes narrowed as she went up to her room. Perhaps she was enjoying his company rather more than was sensible in the circumstances. Holiday romances rarely translated well into everyday life. Not that she could call this a romance, exactly, nor would this man ever be part of her life. Once she left Venice she would never see him again.

With this in mind Laura took longer to get ready than usual. While she was eyeing the limited choice in the wardrobe a flash of lightning preceded a clap of thunder, and she ran to close the open doors on the rain hammering down outside. Choice made, she thought irritably. It had to be the black dress again, but at least she could wear it with the white cotton trench coat packed for just this kind of emergency—very Audrey Hepburn, according to Fen.

Laura had been ready and waiting for several minutes before Domenico rang to say he was in the foyer. When she
hurried down to meet him he gave her the now familiar double kiss of greeting and brandished a tall black umbrella.

'You see, Laura? It is not always moonlight in Venice!'

'And when it rains it certainly rains,' she agreed.

In the doorway Domenico put up the umbrella, then with
his usual *'Permesso'* slid an arm round her waist. 'If you
wish to stay dry we must walk close together. Which makes
me very happy,' he added in her ear.

Laura chuckled, feeling quite happy about it herself. 'Do
we walk very far?'

'No. The restaurant is so near I thought you would not
mind a walk in the rain.'

Held close against Domenico, she didn't mind at all. All
too soon for Laura they entered an alley so narrow they had
to keep very close together indeed before he ushered her into
the large, luxurious interior of a restaurant divided into two
parts, one very sleek and cosmopolitan, the other more rustic,
with a stone fireplace and windows looking out onto a court-
yard.

'I thought you would prefer the room with the true Italian
atmosphere,' said Domenico as a waiter hurried to relieve
him of Laura's raincoat.

'You were right, I do,' she assured him, thanking her lucky
stars as she took in her surroundings that she could rely on
her credit card to pay the bill. Because whatever it cost she
was going to pay for their meal.

'It is not crowded yet as early as this,' he told her, and
looked at her in silence for a moment, something new in his
eyes as they moved over her face.

'What is it?' she asked.

'You glow tonight, Laura.'

'You look pretty good yourself,' she said, smiling.

'*Grazie!*' Domenico pushed the menus aside. '*Allora*, tonight the choice is simple if you like fish.'

'I love it.'

'Good. This restaurant is famous for its *frittura mista dipesce*, a platter of many varieties of fish,' he added. 'You will like it.'

He was right. But though the meal was delicious, and the surroundings elegant, Laura knew very well that most of her pleasure was down to the man who made it so flatteringly plain he delighted in her company.

'It is hard to believe,' he said, when they were drinking coffee, 'that we have known each other so short a time. I wish that you could stay longer, Laura.'

'So do I,' she said regretfully, 'but in three days I fly back to London, and so far I haven't been inside the Basilica, visited the Guggenheim, taken a trip to Murano, or any of the things I was told were a must on holiday in Venice.'

'We shall do that tomorrow.'

Laura's eyes widened. 'But what about your job?'

'I have arranged a little holiday. Until your flight home my time is yours. But now,' he added, a glint of steel in his eyes, 'we come to the difficult moment. Laura, I am known here in Venice. I cannot allow a lady to pay for dinner. So I will settle the bill, *per favore*. If you must,' he added as she opened her mouth to protest, 'you can pay me in private later.'

'Oh, very well,' she said, resigned. 'But just make sure you keep the bill for me.'

'Of course I will,' he said, looking injured. 'Why do you not trust me, Laura?'

She smiled in sudden remorse. 'I do trust you. I just can't let you spend so much money on me.'

'But it is customary for a man to do this when he asks a woman to dine with him. I cannot believe that this is different in London.' Comprehension dawned in his eyes. 'But of course! I am a fool. You think I will expect—'

'*No!* I most certainly do not,' she retorted, colouring.

'You say it is the problem with the men who work in your bank,' he pointed out.

'You're different.'

He raised an eyebrow. 'In what way? I am a man.'

'I know that,' she said, exasperated. 'But it never occurred to me that you'd want—expect—'

'I do not *expect* to make love to you,' Domenico said very quietly, leaning nearer. 'But I would lie if I said I did not want to.' He signalled to the waiter for the bill, paid it, received Laura's raincoat and held it for her, then escorted her outside into the narrow alley.

Nothing was said other than a *'Permesso'* from Domenico as he put his arm round her under the umbrella, but once they left the narrow alley he halted, looking down into her face as the rain teemed down around them.

'We dined early tonight, Laura.'

She was well aware of that. Yet now there seemed no alternative to a return to the Locanda, where there was no bar, or visitors' lounge. 'I need to settle up for dinner,' she reminded him with sudden inspiration.

'That would be difficult here in such rain. And I still have your shopping,' he reminded her. 'I would ask you back to my apartment to collect it, but after our conversation in the restaurant you will suspect my motives, yes?'

She shook her head, smiling. 'No, I won't, Domenico. I'd love to go back to your place.'

After the drenching rain of the not-quite-dark of the lagoon night Domenico's *salotto* glowed with welcome from lamps that threw light on the high white cornices and sparked muted gleams from a collection of mirrors in different sizes, all of them old with carved, gilded frames, some of them in need of restoration.

'I noticed yesterday that there were mirrors instead of pictures,' said Laura as he took her raincoat.

'I am not so *very* vain,' he said, grinning. 'The glass is original in my entire collection; which means it is almost too dim to give a reflection.'

'They're beautiful.'

He held out his hand. 'Come. Sit down, Laura, and let me give you a drink.'

'I don't suppose you have any tea?' she said without hope.

Domenico smiled in smug triumph. 'I bought some today, but I do not drink tea, so it is best you make it yourself.'

'Wonderful!'

In the small kitchen he handed her a packet of teabags labelled 'English Breakfast'. 'It is a little late for breakfast, but I thought you would like this.'

'I'll love it,' she assured him as he filled the kettle. 'Do you have any milk?'

'Of course! I knew that tea would be no use to my charming English guest without it. But there is lemon, if you prefer,' he added.

'You've thought of everything. Thank you.' She gave him a radiant smile.

'Such a smile will gain you anything you wish,' he told her, watching as she poured boiling water on the teabag.

'At this moment all I want in life is a cup of tea,' she said, and savaged the teabag with a spoon. 'What are you having?'

'A glass of wine. Perhaps you would like one later, also.'

Domenico took a tray into the *salotto* and set it down in front of her, watching indulgently as she sipped her tea with a sigh of bliss.

'I've been suffering withdrawal symptoms.' She laughed at his blank look and explained that three days without tea was a personal best for her.

'But why did you not say?' he demanded, sitting beside her. 'We can provide you with tea in any café in Venice.'

'I love the coffee here so much I never thought to ask for tea.' She gave an admiring glance at the *gros point* embroidery on the cushions. 'I envy you these, Domenico.'

He smiled, pleased. 'They are my mother's work.'

'She's very clever. I'm not at all talented when it comes to sewing.'

'Can you cook?'

'It all depends,' she said guardedly.

He looked amused. 'On what, exactly?'

'Your idea of a good meal. Can you cook?'

'Of course,' he said matter-of-factly.

'I thought all Italian males were spoilt rotten by their *mammas*!'

'Often this is true,' he admitted. 'But when I am here in the apartment I sometimes like to make a meal. It is a change for me.'

'And in the hotel?'

'I eat hotel meals,' he said, shrugging.

She eyed him curiously. 'What exactly do you do in this hotel of yours?'

'I work very hard!' He smiled. '*Allora*, would you like more tea, or shall I give you a glass of wine?'

Laura shook her head. 'Nothing more, thanks. But if you'd be kind enough to hand over those bags I left behind I'd love to gloat over my purchases.'

Domenico deposited her shopping at her feet, smiling at her pleasure as she examined her trophies.

'With your help I spent a lot less and bought far more than I expected,' she told him with satisfaction. 'But I also need a proper wedding present for Fen Dysart. I'd like to buy her some Venetian glass—something special.'

'Then we shall go to Murano tomorrow. A reproduction of something old would be good, yes?'

'Perfect.' Laura hesitated. 'As long as they accept credit cards.'

'Of course. They will also ship anything you wish to England.'

'That would be marvellous.' She turned to look him in the eye. '*Allora*, as you Italians say, give me the bill for the meal, please.'

'I hoped you had forgotten.' Domenico sighed heavily. 'I do not like this.'

'Tough. I insist.'

'You are a hard woman.'

'You'd better believe it!' She smiled at him to soften her words, and managed not to wince at the total when he produced the bill from his wallet.

'But remember this, Laura,' he said very deliberately. 'You may pay this one time since it matters so much to you, but that is all. It is understood?'

She nodded meekly, and counted out a pile of euros, relieved to discover she had enough to cover it.

'Do you feel better now?' he demanded.

'Much better,' she assured him, and smiled. 'I think I would like a glass of wine after all.'

'Do you insist on paying when you dine with men in London?' he asked, handing a glass to her.

'That's different,' she said firmly. 'You've not only paid for meals, you've taken time off from your job to help me.'

'Let us talk no more of money.' He sat down beside her. 'Instead, I will make a confession which will amuse you very much.'

'Confession? That sounds serious.'

'It is comical, not serious,' he assured her. 'I will start from the beginning. Last night I was not pleased to find you gone when I went to your hotel.'

'I was afraid of that,' she admitted. 'But, Domenico, you didn't put a phone number on your note, and I couldn't sit for hours twiddling my thumbs in my room when Venice was out there, luring to me to come out and play, now could I?'

'No, of course not.' He smiled and took her hand. 'But when Signora Rossi gave me your message—'

'You were pretty ticked off,' she teased.

'*E vero*, if that means annoyed,' he agreed. 'I had planned the evening so carefully, you understand, and it was not part of the plan to find you gone when I came for you. But when I saw you sitting there at Florian's I was angry no longer. You looked so beautiful—and I was not the only man who thought so,' he added darkly.

She brushed that aside. 'So tell me about this plan.'

'To explain I must go back to our first meeting, when you did not notice me at all!'

She shook her head. 'I did, you know—mainly because you were in such a hurry to get rid of me. But also because you looked respectable and had been sent by Lorenzo Forli—'

'Respectable? *Dio!*' He shook his head in mock despair. 'Women usually have more flattering things to say of me than that, Laura.'

'I bet they do!'

'I met a friend in the San Marco *sestiere* later that day,' he went on, 'and on impulse afterwards I decided to make sure all was well with you. Signora Rossi told me you had gone to Florian's, but when I looked for you there I did not recognise you at first.'

'I clean up well,' she agreed, and Domenico gave a delighted laugh.

'Very well indeed.' He smiled crookedly. 'Until that moment my plan was merely to ask if the hotel was satisfactory—'

'And bowl me over with your charm!' she accused.

'*Esattamente.*' He nodded, unrepentant. 'But after meeting with you it was I who was bowled over, Laura. I enjoyed our time together very much—until you refused my escort back to the hotel.'

'That offended you?'

'I was hurt!' he said, hand on heart. 'I wanted very much to see you again. But to avoid another rejection I sent a note.'

'Very clever,' said Laura, grinning.

'I think so,' he said smugly. '*Allora*, the next part of my plan was to impress you with dinner at Harry's Bar.'

'Excellent move.'

'But during the meal I learned of your dislike of romantic gestures,' he said with a heavy sigh, 'so I abandoned my plan and gave money to one of the waiters to pay off the *gondoliere*. Instead of taking you on a moonlit gondola ride I walked with you back to your hotel.'

Laura stared at him for a moment, then began to laugh helplessly. 'My story about the proposal lost me a trip in a gondola?'

Domenico nodded, grinning. 'But if you wish for one some other time this can be arranged.'

'No, thanks. Besides—' She hesitated.

'Besides?' he prompted.

'Our walk back by moonlight was more to my taste.'

His eyes gleamed. 'You include the kiss?'

She nodded, smiling. 'Short but sweet.'

'I used much self-control,' he said virtuously.

'I was impressed. Your plan worked like a charm without the gondola, Domenico.'

His hand tightened on hers. 'Today there was no plan.'

'And I've enjoyed every minute of it.'

'Even the walk in the rain?'

Laura smiled. 'Especially that.' She leaned nearer and held up her face. 'It's still raining out there so you'd better kiss me goodnight right here.'

To her astonishment Domenico jumped up, shaking his head. 'No.'

Laura stared blankly. 'No?'

'I did not bring you here for that.'

'For what?' She jumped to her feet, eyes cold. 'A kiss is the only thing on offer!'

'I know this,' he said roughly. 'Come. I will take you back.' He strode out of the room, leaving her to stow her shopping away in the bags, all her pleasure in the evening gone. Domenico returned, wearing a black leather jacket, and in silence she thrust her arms into the sleeves of the raincoat he held out.

'It is too wet to take your presents tonight,' he informed her. 'I shall bring them in the morning when I come for you.'

'Are you still going to do that?' she demanded, tying her belt viciously tight.

He frowned. 'Of course. Unless,' he added with sudden hauteur, 'you no longer want me to spend the day with you.'

'Do *you* want to?'

'You know very well that I do.' He took her by the shoulders, the blue eyes darkening as they bored down into hers. 'Try to understand. My instructions were to take care of you. So I am taking you back to your hotel.'

'Message received, loud and clear.' She marched out of the room and down the smooth, worn stone stairs, and at the entrance waited, face averted, while Domenico put up the umbrella. He stood looking down into her set face for a moment then slid his arm round her and held her very firmly.

'It is necessary to share the umbrella,' he informed her.

Still smarting from his rejection, Laura controlled a childish urge to shove him away but held herself poker-stiff, wishing she'd brought her own umbrella as they walked in silence Domenico was the first to break.

'You are very angry with me?' he demanded at last, his accent more noticeable than usual.

'Hurt as well as angry,' she informed him. 'The one time I actually offer to kiss a man he turns me down.'

'I wanted the kiss so much I dared not take it,' he said tightly. 'I am not made of stone, Laura.' He halted in the deserted *calle* as they came in sight of the hotel, holding her closer in the shadows between the lights. 'Here it is different,' he whispered, his breath warm against her cheek.

Laura breathed in the scent of leather and cologne and man as the rain teemed down around them, enclosing them in a private world under the umbrella. His arm tightened and she held up her face as he bent his head to kiss her. Their lips met in a gentle, exploratory caress, which quickly flared into something so different that in some corner of her brain Laura marvelled at Domenico's skill at keeping the umbrella upright as he kissed her with a mounting passion she responded to helplessly, her hands tunnelling under his jacket to hold him closer. At last he gave a smothered groan and raised his head a fraction, his breath hot against her cheek as he held her hard against him.

'Now you see?' he said, in a voice husky with emotion.

'Yes,' she whispered shakily.

Outside the closed door of the hotel Domenico kissed her again, then released her with reluctance.

'*Buona notte*, Laura. Until tomorrow.'

CHAPTER THREE

LAURA woke with the memory of the kisses still warm on her lips. A tendency to gaze into space held her up so much as she got ready that Domenico had already arrived when she ran downstairs. He gave her his usual double kiss of greeting and exchanged a few words with Signora Rossi before sweeping Laura out into the steamy, sunlit warmth of the Venice morning.

'How are you today, *cara*?' he enquired as they went in search of breakfast. 'Did you sleep well?'

'No,' she said frankly. 'Did you?'

He shook his head, sighing. 'I lay awake listening to the rain and thinking of our kisses.'

'Snap!'

He laughed and took her hand. 'I know this now. I am glad you felt the same.'

After a leisurely breakfast Laura insisted they caught a *vaporetto* instead of an expensive water taxi for the short journey to Murano and stood at the rail within Domenico's sheltering arm watching the island come nearer, its outline softened and blurred by the saline lagoon climate.

As they drew up alongside he pointed out the island's ancient canalside porticoes. 'Some of these have survived from mediaeval times, when Murano was the principal glassmaking centre of Europe and its citizens were the only craftsmen in the world able to produce a mirror.'

'A pretty vital invention from a woman's point of view!'

He smiled and smoothed a lock of hair back from her forehead as they left the boat. '*Allora*, before making your choice do you wish to watch our celebrated glass-blowers at work?'

'I certainly do,' she assured him.

'But afterwards, if you see something you like, leave all bargaining to me,' he advised.

When they reached a door with a *'fornace'* sign they went inside to watch a demonstration of the ancient craft that had made Murano famous. Laura watched, fascinated, as the glass blower took a blob of molten paste on the end of an iron rod, and with a skilled, dangerous-looking process of twisting, turning and blowing transformed it into a perfect wine goblet.

'Amazing, Domenico,' she said as they began a tour of the showroom afterwards. 'It's probably all in a day's work to that man, and nothing new to you, but it looked like pure magic to me.'

'With you at my side, Laura, everything in Venice is new to me also,' he said, smiling down at her as she looked at the dazzling array of glass artefacts. 'Have you something in mind for your friend's bride gift? What type of house will she live in?'

'Her fiancé originally bought a flat in a beautiful Georgian house in Pennington, but he now owns the entire property.' She gestured at some extravagantly modern pieces. 'Those are wonderful from a technical point of view, but I want something more traditional, to suit their house.'

Laura would have found it hard to resist the pressure from some of the sales staff on her own, but with Domenico on hand they were left in peace to browse.

'Would she like these?' he asked, pointing at a display of candlesticks and candelabra. *'Millefiori* is not everyone's taste, but perhaps she would like the *aventurine*, which uses gold.'

Laura nodded enthusiastically. 'Exactly Fen's sort of thing.'

After lengthy deliberation on style and cost, she eventually chose a pair of tall candlesticks with hair-fine strands of gold twined through their serpentine, tactile curves. Domenico did some efficient haggling, which brought the price down considerably, but in the end Laura decided against having them shipped.

'Just in case they don't arrive in time for the wedding,' she told him. 'I must have my present ready for the big day. Thanks a lot for the expert bargaining.'

He smiled, and took charge of the gift as they went to catch the *vaporetto* back to San Marco. 'So. I have my uses!'

'Oh, very definitely,' she assured him, 'one of which is to tell me who is on the other pillar.'

'Cosa?' he said blankly.

'At the entrance to San Marco. The lion of Venice is on one pillar, but who stands on the other one?'

'Ah! That is San Teodoro,' he said, enlightened. 'Saint Theodore to you. And be warned: superstitious Venetians never walk between the pillars because in the past executions took place there. And now,' he added, 'I have a confession to make.'

'Another one?' she said, laughing.

'I went early to the market this morning, and in my hurry afterwards I forgot your shopping again.'

'Never mind, I can pick it up on my way back to the hotel.'

'And we shall eat lunch at the apartment. Or we can go out, of course,' he added quickly.

'I prefer your apartment.' She smiled at him as they left the boat. 'I like it very much, Domenico.'

'Do you like me very much, also?' he asked, so utterly serious Laura gave him a startled look.

'Yes, I do.'

'Bene!' he said with satisfaction, and took her hand. 'Do not worry. I shall not drop the *candeliere.'*

Laura volunteered to make an omelette to accompany the bread and salad Domenico had bought fresh that morning, and after sizing up the cooker and the pan he gave her she uttered a silent prayer and got to work with butter, eggs and herbs. Domenico watched in approval as for the final touch she gave the pan a brisk shake, folded the omelette in half, and slid two crisp, soft-centred portions onto the plates he had ready.

'*Perfetto,*' he assured her as they began eating.

'You're being kind,' she told him, delighted that her effort had turned out so well.

'No, I am truthful.' He smiled as he helped her to salad. 'The *frittata* is delicious and so is the chef. This is a very special occasion for me. Except for my mother no woman has ever offered to make lunch for me here.'

Laura didn't want to hear about other women in Domenico's apartment. 'You can make me some tea as my reward,' she told him.

'Of course,' he said, and laid a peeled peach on her plate. 'But afterwards you must do as we Venetians do and rest for a while before we go on with the day. So this afternoon is it to be the Guggenheim or the Basilica? I do not advise both.'

'The Basilica. Let's do ancient today and modern tomorrow—if you still have time to spare for tomorrow?' she added, flushing.

'My time is yours until you leave,' he reminded her as he got up to make her tea. 'Which is not long now. You must come back again soon, Laura.'

'Not possible, I'm afraid. I won't be able to afford another trip to Venice for quite a while,' she said with regret.

He frowned as he put a teabag in a cup. 'If cost is a problem I could—'

'No, you couldn't, Domenico,' she said gently.

Instead of arguing, as she'd half expected, he made her tea, added milk, and gave her the cup. 'First you drink this tea, then you rest in the *salotto*.'

'I want to help clear up,' she objected.

'No, *cara*—you did the cooking,' he said firmly. 'Is the tea to your taste?'

It was too weak and milky by far, but Laura assured him it was delicious and drank every drop. Afterwards she spent a few minutes on repairs in the bathroom, then made for the window in the sitting room to look down at the water traffic on the sunlit water below, amused as she contrasted it with her daily commute in London.

'You smile like the *Mona Lisa*,' said Domenico behind her.

She turned to him. 'I was looking at all these people travelling about on the water in the sunshine—a bit different from my daily trips on the Docklands Light Railway.'

'This train is convenient for your apartment?'

She nodded. 'I live in a part of London called Bow, so the DLR, as we locals call it, is almost door to door from my flat to the bank.'

He took her hand in his and drew her down to sit beside him. 'Tell me about your flat, Laura.'

'It's very small, with only one bedroom, and very different from this. But on the plus side it's in a building with a gym and a pool. I've been very grateful for both assets since the downward turn in my social life.' She yawned suddenly. 'Sorry. It must be the Venice air.'

'Come, it is early yet. Put your head on that cushion and enjoy a short *siesta*. Then later we shall tour the Basilica.'

Laura found it all too easy to do as he said. She curled up in her corner of his sofa, so utterly at ease now in Domenico's company that she was soon asleep.

He sat back, resisting the urge to stroke the gleaming braid trailing over Laura's shoulder. He looked at her flushed, sleeping face, the desire he could not ignore mixed with a protective feeling new to him in his dealings with women. When Lorenzo Forli had requested—no, ordered him to take care of Fenella's friend he had never imagined in his wildest dreams that she would appeal to him so strongly.

He sat very still as she stirred, but she merely turned her face deeper into the cushion, and he let out a deep breath and relaxed. In the years since Alessa's desertion, which had cut deeper and hurt for much longer than he had allowed anyone to know, his dealings with women had been light-hearted, casual affairs conducted discreetly, with no involve-ment of the heart, and in some cases, he thought wryly, of the brain, either. But Laura was different. He desired her as a lover, as was only natural, but he also liked and respected her as a person. Unlike this idiot Edward of hers, he would not reject friendship if she offered it. But it took self-control he had not known he possessed to keep from touching her.

Laura woke slowly, and found a pair of intent blue eyes watching her. 'Hello,' she said sleepily. 'Did I snore?'

Domenico shook his head, smiling. Ignoring an urge to devour her flushed face with kisses, he got up, holding out his hand. 'Come, I shall take you back to the hotel.'

Laura would have preferred to stay right where she was for the foreseeable future, but with a sigh she took the hand and let him pull her to her feet. 'I need a shower and a change of clothes.'

'This is a good idea,' he said with approval. 'Then you will have no need to return to your hotel after the Basilica. We shall go to Florian's instead, and while you drink tea there you shall tell me where you would like to dine this evening.'

'Perfect.' She hesitated. 'But I'm going back to the hotel on my own, right now, Domenico. I'll meet you in an hour outside the central doorway of the Basilica.'

He dropped her hand. 'Very well, if that is what you wish.'

'I just need to do a little shopping on my own—personal things,' she explained, her colour rising.

'Ah. I see. Of course.' He opened the door for her and

accompanied her down to the foyer, where he kissed her cheeks and tapped her watch. 'One hour. I shall be waiting.'

Laura went straight to a shop she'd seen the day before. She picked out a silk tie with discreet aquamarine dots printed on a midnight-blue background, handed over her credit card and hurried with her gift-wrapped purchase through the now-familiar alleys to the Locanda Verona.

She rushed through a shower with her head wrapped in a towel, did her face, and took a look through her limited wardrobe for something suitable for both a visit to the Basilica and to a restaurant somewhere afterwards. The only dress still unworn was brand-new, a chain-store bargain bought for Tuscany, with drifts of tawny butterflies printed on double layers of cream chiffon. Definitely not for church, Laura decided with regret, and put on a fluted cream linen skirt and a thin, lace-edged black cardigan she was buttoning up to the low V-neck when her phone rang.

'I am here, with your parcels at last,' said Domenico. 'Are you ready?'

Oh, yes, she was ready. 'I'll be right down.'

Laura ran down the stairs, smiling, her heart lifting at the sight of Domenico leaning against the reception desk in pale linen trousers and one of his blue shirts.

'Here is your shopping, *signorina*,' he said, and gave her the bags first and then the box containing the candlesticks. 'Go up more slowly than you came down,' he advised, 'or you will endanger the *candeliere*.'

Laura meekly went back up the stairs at a slower rate, which was an effort when she wanted nothing more than to race up and down to get back to Domenico as fast as she could; a disturbing thought when all too soon she would be waving him a permanent goodbye.

'I thought we were meeting outside the Basilica,' she said, when she rejoined him.

'I finally remembered your presents. Also,' he added, giv-

ing her a head-to-toe survey, 'I did not think it wise to leave
you waiting in the *piazza* alone, and I was right. You look
more beautiful each time I see you.'

Laura knew perfectly well she wasn't beautiful, but had a
feeling she might start believing it herself if she spent much
more time in Domenico's company. 'You look rather nice,
too,' she said as they left the hotel.

'I did my best just for you,' he said suavely, and grinned
at the look she gave him.

'How do you manage to find shirts the exact shade of your
eyes?' she asked as they strolled along the *calle*.

'There are many blue shirts sold in Venice, Laura. I was
not aware of trying to match my eyes,' he protested.

'I don't believe you! You know to a scintilla the effect
your eyes have on a woman.'

'Do they affect you?' he demanded, stopping to look down
at her.

'Oh, yes—but I'm working on it,' she said, laughing.

'If it is any satisfaction to you, Laura, your eyes have a
much greater effect on me. So does your mouth,' he said
conversationally as they resumed walking. 'And your hair.
Also I have great affection for your pretty ears and your—'

'Stop it!' she ordered sternly. 'We're visiting a place of
worship, remember.'

'And we must hurry.' Domenico looked at his watch as
they dived into the tide of tourists. 'The Basilica will be fully
lit only until four o'clock.'

Laura had read up a little about the Basilica beforehand,
but when they passed through the carved central doorway to
mount the steps into the cathedral itself she was unprepared
for the sheer impact of gleaming golden mosaics on every
inch of the huge interior: domes, walls and floor, from the
vestibule right through the nave. The effect was so stunning
that in some ways she was glad there were the usual crowds.

They made progress slow, but lessened her feeling of personal insignificance in the overwhelming golden vastness.

'I had no idea,' she said to Domenico as she looked down at the floor mosaics, which undulated beneath her feet like an exotic Eastern carpet.

'I had forgotten, too, it is years since I was here,' he said quietly, holding her firmly by the hand as they moved on through the crowd. 'Look up.'

Laura obeyed, gazing up into the gleaming Pentecost dome at the sight of the Apostles touched by tongues of flame. But under the enormous central dome of the Ascension she was rendered utterly silent by the glittering gold mosaic of Christ in Glory high above.

'Come,' said Domenico. 'We must buy tickets to view the Pala d'Oro.'

By the time Laura had admired the tomb of St Mark and the Pala d'Oro, the bejewelled gold altarpiece behind the high altar, she had the beginnings of a headache. Domenico looked at her with concern when she took refuge behind her enormous sunglasses.

'Come, *tesoro*. Enough for now, yes?'

Laura nodded silently as they made their way back through the crowds in the Basilica to emerge into the thronged, sunlit *piazza*. 'It's an amazing building, but a bit of it at a time is more than enough. It needs a few visits to take it all in.'

'When you come back we shall see it again, but early in the morning, before the crowds arrive,' he promised. 'And there is the Doge's Palace to see, also.'

At that moment the very thought of it made her tired. 'Domenico, could we just have tea at your place instead of Florian's?' said Laura. 'I have a bit of a headache. I don't think I could face an orchestra right now.'

'But of course.' He looked down into her colourless face. 'Shall we call at a *farmacia* for some medication?'

'I've got some painkillers with me.' She smiled at him

gratefully. 'I just need lots of water and lots of tea, and peaceful surroundings without tourists or a single gold mosaic.'

'Then my apartment is the perfect place!'

Laura was in full agreement later as she sank into one of the sofas in the cool, high-ceilinged *salotto* to sip the tea Domenico had made stronger and darker than before.

'I did not think you enjoyed my former effort,' he said, sitting beside her. 'But you were too polite to say so.'

'This time it's perfect,' she assured him, and with a little grin, said *'Permesso?'* and toed her sandals off so she could curl up in her corner of the sofa.

Domenico gave her a look that made her heart skip a beat. 'For me, Laura, this is much, much better than Florian's.'

'For me, too,' she said, taking refuge in her tea. 'After the pills and all that mineral water you made me wash them down with, my headache is better already.'

'That is because you are here with me,' he said, with such smug certainty she laughed.

'You're outrageous.'

He looked wounded. 'Not at all. I meant that here where it is quiet and cool and there are no tourists—and where you are served with such wonderful tea—you naturally feel better.'

Laura smiled warmly. 'Of course I do. Thank you, Domenico.'

'Prego. Now, let us decide where to dine tonight.'

'We could go to your hotel,' she said slyly.

'No!' he said, with such emphasis her eyebrows rose.

'Why not?'

He threw out a hand. 'This is a holiday for me, also, Laura, and I do not wish to dine in the place where I spend most of my working life. Also I would have to introduce you to many people and waste much time that could be spent alone with you. When you come back I shall take you there. But not this time.'

'I can't manage another trip to Venice for quite a while, you know,' she said with a sigh.

He shot her a searching look. 'I know cost has been mentioned before, but if it is a matter of money—'

'Of course it is. I earn quite a good salary, but a lot of it goes on rent.' She looked away. 'I also help my mother out a bit—a very little bit—with my sister Abby's college fund.'

'Because you have no father?' he said with sympathy, and put her cup on the table so he could hold her hand.

'Right. My mother teaches in the local primary school, and Abby works in a café at weekends to add her bit to the fund, but I want her to have a reasonable nest egg in the bank by the time she goes to college. This holiday of mine was pure extravagance right now. I would never have made it here if you hadn't found such a cheap place for me to stay.' Laura turned to look at him. 'It was you who arranged it?'

He nodded, and raised her hand to his lips. 'And because his request led to our meeting, Laura, I shall be grateful to Signor Forli for the rest of my life.'

CHAPTER FOUR

'THAT'S a very extravagant thing to say,' said Laura, after a pause.

'It is true. If it had not been for him I would have sent someone else to the airport to meet you.' Domenico gave her a wry smile. 'It is not usually my—my job to do such things.'

'Is that why you were in such a strop at the airport?'

'Strop?'

'Temper.'

He shrugged. 'I had problems at the hotel that day, and was forced to leave them unresolved to meet you at Marco Polo. I apologise for my bad manners.'

She grinned. 'I took no notice.'

'I know it. You were so entranced with Venice you took no notice of me at all,' he said darkly, his hand tightening on hers. 'My self-esteem suffered a crushing blow.'

'I'm glad.'

'You are *glad*?'

'Otherwise you wouldn't have come after me to make sure I did notice you,' she said matter-of-factly. 'And we wouldn't be here right now, enjoying each other's company.'

He smiled. '*E vero*. For once in my life I rejoice that I was ignored by a woman!'

She looked at him searchingly. 'Domenico, is your effect on women really so important to you?'

He shrugged, the smile suddenly bitter. 'If I say yes will you understand?'

Laura noted the pulse throbbing at the corner of his mouth and chose her words with care. 'It dates from the day Alessa left you for your friend?'

His eyes lit up. 'You do understand!'

'I know how the bottom can fall out of one's world.'

'Did some man do this to you, Laura?' he demanded, frowning.

'Not in the way you mean. The only man I've ever adored was my father. He died suddenly of a heart attack when I was ten.'

'Poor little one! That must have been very hard for you.'

She nodded sadly. 'But much harder for my mother. I realise now how wonderfully she coped with it all. She had to bury her own grief to comfort Abby and me, move us into a smaller house, and go back to work to support us.'

'She must be a very special lady. Life changed very much for her, and for you,' he said with sympathy.

Laura shrugged. 'Children are adaptable. I was inconsolable at first, but in time I realised that as long as I had my mother and Abby I could cope, too. The other constant in my life was Fen, of course. I've always been treated like one of the family by the Dysarts.' She smiled to lighten the atmosphere. 'I'm chief bridesmaid at the wedding.'

'Are there many such bridesmaids?'

'Three besides me. Fen's teenage nieces, you probably know one of them—Francesca Forli.'

'I do, yes, but at this moment I am interested only in you,' said Domenico firmly. 'Tell me what you will wear, Laura, so I can picture you in my mind.'

'Better still, I'll send you a photograph—if you like.'

'I would like that very much.' He eyed her closely. 'And now that you look better, Laura, let us talk of where you would like to dine tonight.'

She hesitated. 'Domenico—could we possibly stay in and eat something here?'

'You may do anything you wish,' he assured her.

'Do they do takeaways in Venice? If not, a sandwich will do.'

'I can give you something better than a *tramezzino*!'

'You're going to cook?'

'You cannot imagine such a thing?' he teased, and brandished his mobile phone. 'I shall persuade one of the chefs at the hotel to send us a cold meal of some kind.'

'Wonderful!'

'Can you eat shellfish?'

'Any kind you like.'

'Then I shall ring Sandro to see what he can do.' Domenico looked down at her as he got up. 'You feel better now, *cara*?'

'Much better. But, Domenico, if you prefer to go out—'

'I do not,' he said with emphasis. 'We shall sit on the little balcony outside the dining room while we wait for our dinner, and watch the boats on the Canalazzo.'

'Canalazzo?' Laura queried.

'You foreigners call it the Grand Canal!' he said, laughing.

The minute the door closed behind him Laura went to the window to gaze at the baroque splendour of the Salute church across the lagoon. She heaved a sigh. She had been here only a short time, yet she would miss Venice when she was back in London. She would miss Domenico a whole lot more— but she wasn't going to think about that.

It was some time before he rejoined her. 'You should be resting,' he accused.

'My headache has vanished completely,' she assured him, and smiled. 'You know I can't resist this view.'

He smiled indulgently. 'Then let us go outside to see more of it.'

Domenico's balcony was narrow, with only room for a table and four chairs, but the view from it was spectacular. Laura leaned against the rail, watching the assorted water traffic, and wished she could paint as she watched a gondola trail a glittering wake on the water below.

'The passengers are tourists, of course,' said Domenico,

leaning beside her. 'The only time Venetians travel by gondola is on their wedding day.'

'So you were going to make an exception for me the other night, then!'

He slanted a smile at her. 'I was determined to impress you.'

'You would have succeeded!' She leaned farther to watch the gondola out of sight. 'I'm disappointed, Domenico. I hoped he would serenade his passengers.'

He laughed. 'This does not happen. The only melodies uttered by *gondoliere* are the warning calls heard on our canals for centuries.'

'Another illusion shattered!'

'Let me console you with wine.'

'I'd better stick to water just yet, please.'

Left alone again, Laura gazed in concentration at the view from the balcony, so she would remember every detail of it when life resumed normal service back in London. She turned with a smile as Domenico came back with a loaded tray.

'*Allora*, we have wine, San Pellegrino, fresh fruit juice and ice,' he announced. 'I thought you might like a taste of peach and orange in your mineral water, Laura.'

'I would indeed,' she agreed. 'You're very good to me, Domenico.'

He shot a narrowed, gleaming look at her. 'When you smile at me like so it is not easy to be very good.'

'Then I won't.'

'Which would be a pity.'

Their eyes held for a moment, then Domenico turned away to toss ice in a glass. He added a mixture of fruit juice and mineral water, topped it off with lemon slices and handed the drink to her with a bow. 'Perhaps the *signorina* will give me her verdict.'

Laura eyed him in admiration. 'You speak such wonderful English, Domenico.'

'*Grazie*. I learned in school, of course, and then later I— I did a more intensive language course and became more fluent. It is necessary in my line of work.' He gestured towards her glass. 'Taste, *cara*.'

Laura took a sip and smiled at him. 'Delicious.'

He poured a glass of wine and took the chair beside her. '*Salute*.'

She raised her glass to him. 'To you, Domenico, for making my holiday so special.'

'It is not so hard a thing to do,' he assured her, and leaned back in his chair, utterly relaxed.

Laura's eyes were thoughtful as she studied the clear-cut profile etched against the fiery light.

'That is a strange look, Laura,' he said, intercepting it.

She shrugged, smiling. 'It suddenly occurred to me that this time last week we didn't know each other existed.'

'It is hard to believe,' he agreed soberly. 'There is so much I wish to learn about you, *cara*. Tell me more about your family; describe them to me.'

'My mother is small and fair like me, and very attractive—'

'Also like you!'

'Thank you, kind sir. Abby is tall, with dark hair like my father. She's the brains of the family, but no slouch in the looks department, either. She's off to Trinity, Cambridge, in the autumn.'

'That is very impressive.' Domenico shot a look at her. 'It will also be expensive, which is why you help her and why you cannot return soon.' He turned to her, his eyes brilliant with sudden inspiration. 'But I have a solution for this.'

Laura eyed him warily. 'What?'

'You will refuse to let me pay your air fare, I know, but instead of a hotel you could stay here in my apartment as my guest. I will not impose my company on you. You are most welcome to stay here alone, or with your mother and sister, perhaps, any time you wish.'

She smiled at him, deeply touched. 'Domenico, that's such a lovely thought, but I couldn't possibly take advantage of your kindness like that.'

The light vanished from his eyes. 'Why not?' he demanded with sudden hauteur. 'Do not confuse me with these *ragazzi* at your bank. I would ask nothing in return.'

'I know that. Don't go all arrogant and Venetian on me!' She heaved a sigh. 'It's a lovely idea, but just not possible for me right now.'

'As you wish,' he said coolly, and got up at the sound of the doorbell. 'Our dinner.'

Laura bit her lip as she watched him go. She drained her glass and went into the dining room, and with a pang saw that Domenico had made the table festive with candles and crystal and a beautiful linen cloth and napkins. She waited until the outer door closed, then went into the hall to confront him.

'Domenico, I didn't mean to offend you. I would like nothing better than to take you up on your offer, but I just can't make it back to Venice for a while. Please try to understand.'

'Mi dispiace,' he said with instant remorse. 'Of course I understand. Let us talk no more of things which distress you, *cara.*' He took Laura's hand and led her back to the balcony to watch the sun sinking into the lagoon in a blaze of crimson fire.

'It's so lovely here.' She sighed. 'I shall think of this a lot when it's raining back in London.'

'It rains here too. This had great advantages for me last night,' he reminded her, eyes gleaming.

'For me, too,' said Laura, seeing no point in beating about the bush.

'But you were angry with me!'

'Only because you didn't want to kiss me.'

'Laura,' he said impatiently, 'I wanted to kiss you far too much. You have forgotten what happened when I did?'

'No.' She took in a deep, unsteady breath. 'No, I haven't.'

'*Va bene.* Neither have I,' he said with feeling. 'So let us turn our attention to dinner.'

'What are we having?' she asked, wrenching her mind away from the interlude in the rain.

'A special dinner for a special guest. I hope you will enjoy it.'

'I'm sure I will. I've enjoyed everything I've eaten here, right down to the ham *panino* in a bar near the Rialto.'

'I trust that you ate this standing up! Otherwise the cost is doubled.'

'I knew that.' She chuckled. 'I can't tell you what a relief it was to sit down when we had breakfast together.'

He laughed. 'I enjoyed this also in your company. Normally I breakfast alone.'

'In London I don't have any at all.'

'That is not good for one who works hard, *cara*,' he said, frowning.

'I know, but I get up early and just can't face anything at that hour.' She turned to smile up at him. 'But I can face dinner tonight any time you like.'

'Then we shall eat at once.'

Revelling in the domesticity in the situation, Laura followed behind with bread and salad while Domenico transferred an enormous platter of seafood from his refrigerator to the dining room table.

'A smaller version is served as *antipasti*,' he informed her, 'but I thought you would like it as a main course.'

'I certainly will!' Laura watched in awe as he dressed the impressive array with olive oil and lemon juice. 'Lobster, prawns, crab, mussels—but what are the other things, Domenico?'

'Small squid, also various shellfish found only here in the lagoon.' He held a chair for her. 'Sit, *signorina*.' He flicked out one of the linen napkins and laid it over her lap, then filled their wineglasses, and as the final touch lit the candles.

Laura smiled ruefully as he took the seat opposite. 'I'm going to miss all this when I'm scrambling eggs back in London. Think of me now and then at dinner time, Domenico.'

'I shall think of you a great deal more than that!' He looked into her eyes. 'I hope you also will think of me.'

She held his gaze steadily. 'You can safely count on that.'

'Bene.' He smiled. 'Now, let us think no more of meals apart and enjoy the one we are eating together.'

Laura enjoyed it all the more for eating it alone with him as they lingered over the meal. 'This is so much better than a restaurant,' she said with satisfaction. 'Give my compliments to your friend the chef.'

'I will. Though it is not the food that makes the evening special for me, Laura.' Domenico got to his feet, holding out his hand. 'Come, let us sit in the *salotto*.'

'First we clear away,' she said sternly, 'and this time I help.'

'You know I have a machine to wash dishes,' he protested.

'All we need do is load it, then!'

'Are you happy now?' demanded Domenico, when they sat down together later.

She turned to him with a lazy smile. 'Right now I'm very happy indeed.'

He gave a sigh of deep satisfaction. 'I, also. This has been a very good day.'

'Was it strange for you, Domenico? Doing so many tourist things?'

'I enjoyed it very much. With you for company, Laura, how could I not?'

'You say the nicest things!'

He was silent for a while, staring down at his handsome shoes, but at last he drew in a deep breath and turned to her. 'I have something else to say, but perhaps you will not think it so nice.'

'What is it?' she said apprehensively.

His eyes darkened. 'I am in love with you, Laura.'

She sat very still, her heart thumping so loudly she was sure he must be able to hear it.

'Say something, *tesoro*,' he said urgently.

'We've only just met,' she said at last.

'This matters?'

'You can't say it was love at first sight!'

'*E vero!* You were not impressed by me.'

'I was, really,' she confessed. 'When a handsome Italian spoke to me at the airport I was quite excited for a moment—until I realised he was desperate to get rid of me.'

'I came to seek you out afterwards,' he reminded her.

'Only to impress me with your charm and good looks!'

Domenico leaned nearer. 'Did I succeed, *carissima*?'

Her eyes dropped. 'It was good to have company on my first night in Venice.'

'Yet you did not allow me to escort you back to the hotel.'

'You were so sure I'd say yes, I just had to say no,' she said frankly.

He laughed. 'So. I admit I did not fall in love with you at first sight, but I can tell you the exact moment when I did.'

Laura leaned closer. 'When you kissed me that first time?'

'That is when it began, perhaps. But the moment of truth came next morning at the hotel.' He traced a finger down her cheek. 'You ran down the stairs to me, flushed and smiling and so desirable it was a very good thing Signora Rossi was behind her desk.'

She took in a deep, unsteady breath. 'Then why turn me down when I offered to kiss you last night?'

Domenico's fingers tightened on hers. 'I think you know this very well.'

They stared into each other's eyes for a moment. Then as though two giant hands had propelled them together they were in each other's arms, his mouth on hers in a kiss she felt right down to her toes. At the touch of his tongue on hers she responded with such fire Domenico lifted her onto his lap, caressing the curve of her breasts through the thin black fabric, and Laura breathed in sharply, arching into the touch of his hands as his kiss grew fiercer. She shivered in delight when his fingers found bare skin and threw her head back in total abandon as his mouth moved down her throat. When his lips reached the warm hollow between her breasts Domenico was utterly still for a moment before his mouth returned to hers and crushed it with a kiss that made her head reel. Then he set her on her feet and strode to the window, his back turned.

'I will not do this, Laura,' he said hoarsely. 'I want you. *Dio*, how I want you! But if I take you now you will believe I talked of my feelings only to seduce you.'

'You mean you're afraid Lorenzo Forli would sack you if he found out,' she snapped, utterly mortified by another rejection. She caught her breath in dismay as Domenico turned on her, transformed in a heartbeat from lover into a cold, hostile stranger. 'I'm sorry,' she said penitently, backing away. 'That didn't come out the way I intended.'

His smile chilled her to the bone. 'You made your meaning very clear. You are mistaken, however. I have no fear of losing my job. I simply believe it would be wrong to make love to a woman who is not only alone in Venice, but also placed in my care. You come from a different culture, so perhaps this is hard for you to understand. Come. I shall take you back.'

'Domenico—'

He threw up a hand, silencing her very effectively, his eyes hard and cold, like ovals of translucent blue glass. After a tense moment Laura turned away to pick up her handbag and thrust a few straying fronds of hair into place as she fought hard to regain her composure.

When she had command of herself she turned back to him. 'Thank you so much for dinner, and the help you've given me during my holiday,' she said, frigidly polite. 'But please don't trouble yourself to walk back with me. I prefer to return alone.'

He brushed this aside with hauteur. '*Non importa*, I shall see you back to the hotel.'

The look in Domenico's eyes was so implacable Laura turned away and made for the door he held open for her. They went downstairs and out into the *calle* in silence, which lasted, unbroken, all the way to the Locanda Verona.

Afraid her voice would never make it past the lump in her throat, Laura gave Domenico a silent, regal nod in response to his formal bow and walked without hurry across the bridge and through the open doorway of the hotel. She took her key from Signora Rossi, and with a mute smile of thanks escaped to the sanctuary of her room and closed the door behind her.

CHAPTER FIVE

THE night was endless. Hot and miserable, Laura tossed and turned for hours, embarrassed because her frustrated body refused to give her peace. If this was a side effect of falling in love she was glad she'd never done it before. It was all academic anyway. After throwing the insult at him she would never get the chance to tell Domenico how she felt. Not that it mattered. A relationship of any kind between them was impractical; geographically and every other way. Better to end it now, before any more damage was done.

She sighed in the darkness. Her relationships with men in the past had been light-hearted, uncommitted affairs, with no regrets and no harm done when they were over. Except for Edward. He'd astounded her with the scene at the Ritz because she'd known him since they were children. She regretted the loss of his friendship, but it didn't keep her awake at night. While the thought of never seeing Domenico again was unbearable. Laura swallowed a dry, despairing sob, turned on the light and reached for her guidebook. The visit to the Guggenheim would obviously be made solo now, so she might as well give up trying to sleep and find out how to get there.

Mission accomplished, Laura picked up a paperback and tried her best to read for a while, but the story was so obviously heading for a much happier ending than her own she gave up and switched off the light, then groaned as she remembered the silk tie intended as a parting gift. She would have to find some way to get it to Domenico. Taking it to his apartment was out of the question. She would just have to deliver it to his hotel. Wherever that might be. Domenico had been surprisingly cagey on the subject.

Laura got up early next morning, feeling groggy from lack of sleep and the overdose of emotion. To put her brain in gear she stood in the shower for a while and took a long time over her hair afterwards. When it was brushed and pinned back in a severe twist without a tendril in sight she put on her last clean white T-shirt and pair of jeans, stuffed her guidebook and supply of postcards in her satchel and went downstairs. Once she had steeled herself to deliver the tie she would make for the Guggenheim and a dose of modern art.

Signora Rossi was at her desk, smiling. '*Buon giorno*, Miss Green.'

'Good morning.' Laura smiled awkwardly. 'I'm afraid I've forgotten the name of the hotel where Signor Chiesa works. Would you happen to know it?'

'But of course. It is the Forli Palace,' said the woman, looking surprised.

'Thank you. Is it far from here?'

Supplied with directions, Laura went out for coffee and drank it at a table for once. She looked through her postcards, singled out a view of Florian's outdoor tables, and wrote a brief message on it to enclose with the tie.

> *To Domenico, with thanks for all your kindness, Laura.*

She resealed the gift packaging, wrote his name on the label, finished her coffee and went off to search for the Forli Palace. Following the *signora*'s directions, she crossed the Ponte della Paglia, with its bird's-eye view of the Bridge of Sighs, and joined the teeming crowds on the promenade on the busy Riva degli Schiavoni. People eddied around the busy stalls and hurried to and fro from the *vaporetto* stops, but Laura's interest was centred on the volume of gondolas, tugs, water buses and taxis on the waters of the lagoon, with even a naval ship just visible in the distance. Eventually the crowds thinned out and Laura reached a row of *palazzos* long since converted into luxury hotels. Her heart sank when she found the Forli Palace, which was as unlike the Locanda Verona as a hotel could possibly be. The foyer was all pillars, mirrors and frescoes, with great urns of flowers, chandeliers of Venetian glass, and an expanse of marble floor to cross to reach a reception desk manned not by Domenico, to her huge relief, but by two young men who smiled courteously as she approached.

Laura said good morning very firmly in English and held out the package to one of them in response to an offer of help. 'For Signor Domenico Chiesa,' she said briefly.

'Did you wish to see him, *signorina*?'

'No! No, that won't be necessary,' she said hastily. 'But would you make sure that he receives this fairly soon, please?'

'*Senza fallo!* Without fail,' he repeated. 'I will personally make sure of this. But I require your name, please, *signorina*.'

'Miss Laura Green,' she said formally. '*Grazie.*'

Her duty done, Laura squared her shoulders and set off on the longish walk to Dorsoduro to explore the Guggenheim, the one-storey *palazzo* that from the picture in her guidebook looked out of place among the other buildings in Venice. With Domenico for company she would have travelled by water taxi, but for her remaining time in Venice her diminishing finances meant a walk everywhere. The morning was hot, and the combination of a sleepless night and the nervous strain of visiting the Forli Palace had depleted her energy level to the point that when she'd crossed the Accademia Bridge and found the museum her enthusiasm for modern art, or any other kind, was at low ebb. She brightened a little when she found that the young guide who offered help at the Guggenheim actually came from London, but because of this had to pretend interest she didn't feel. After a detailed tour of works by familiar names like Picasso, Mondriaan and Ernst, others by artists Laura had never heard of, plus a whole room devoted to the works of Jackson Pollock, her guide took her round the statuary in the garden. But when they reached the canal entrance a sculpture of a horse bearing a man in a state of full arousal was a statue too many for Laura, and, face burning behind the dark glasses, she muttered her thanks and left in a hurry to go in search of caffeine.

She came to a halt at one of the cafés along the Zattere, where the views across the Giudecca Canal were delightful and the prices a lot cheaper than in San Marco. Lunch seemed like a good idea now she was here, in case she couldn't face the prospect of a solitary dinner later. After a toasted sandwich and some orange juice, followed by an espresso to perk her up, Laura walked back to the hotel, so tired by the time she got there she collapsed on her bed, desperate for sleep. And stayed wide awake. Exasperated, she read for a while instead, but at last gave up, dressed again, and went out to look at some of the Renaissance art Venice was famous for.

During her window-shopping in the Mercerie Laura had noticed a side entrance between the shops to the San Salvatore church and made this her first stop. The beautiful Renaissance interior was impressive, but without Domenico for company Laura felt totally overwhelmed by it, and after only a cursory inspection of the two Titian paintings the guidebook mentioned she went back to the shops. She wandered past the tempting merchandise on display in the windows again for a while, but when she reached Campo Santo Stefano Laura dutifully went inside the church to admire the ship's keel ceiling and marble pillars mentioned in the guidebook. Her duty done, she went back out into the big square and sat down in one of the open-air cafés to cool down with an ice cream. While she waited for it she watched children playing near the central statue and wondered what on earth to do for the rest of the day. But originally she had expected to be alone in Venice for her entire stay. So she would just have to resign herself to spending her last night here with a book in her hotel room or come back to this busy square to eat. It would be too painful to visit Florian's again.

Laura sighed, took out the postcards she'd bought earlier, and began writing messages on them, ready to post on her way back. Halfway through the pile her phone rang, and she seized it, heart thumping, to say a cautious, hopeful hello.

'Laura?'

Her heart leapt at the sound of the voice she'd never expected to hear again.

'Yes?'

'Domenico. I have just received your gift. Many, many thanks. I did not expect this.'

'No, I don't suppose you did. I bought it before we went to the Basilica yesterday.'

'Where are you now?'

'In the square where we found the gold mask.'

'Ah. Campo Santo Stefano.'

'So my guidebook says.'

'Laura, *ascolta*—listen. I know you fly back tomorrow.'

'I leave after breakfast.'

'It is a very bad thing to part in such a way. I was angry last night—'

'You had every right to be. I regretted the words the moment I said them. I apologise.'

'I said certain words that I do not regret,' he said, his voice a tone lower.

Not sure what answer he expected in answer to that, Laura played safe. 'I'm very glad you rang.'

'*Bene*. I am glad also. Laura, let us dine together one last time tonight, yes?'

Oh, yes, *please*! 'Thank you,' she said, deliberately polite to mask the joy bubbling up inside her. 'I'd like that very much.'

'Then I will call for you at seven.'

Laura put the phone away and sat utterly still for a long time, savouring the blissful feeling of relief. Campo Santo Stefano was suddenly the most beautiful place on earth. She no longer felt tired, and tomorrow she would fly home in far happier frame of mind now the parting with Domenico seemed likely to be at least amicable. She rang her mother to confirm that she'd go straight to Stavely for the weekend for Fen's hen party, and then strolled back to the hotel to get ready for the evening. She was in such tearing spirits during the process she was ready and waiting in the airy chiffon dress when the phone rang dead on the minute at seven o'clock.

'I am here,' said Domenico.

'Give me a moment and I'll be right down.'

Laura sprayed a cloud of perfume into the air, walked through it on her way to the door, and then made herself go downstairs at a sedate pace. Her heart missed a beat at the sight of Domenico in the reception hall, which was deserted for once. He wore a formal dark suit with a gleaming white shirt and the tie she'd bought, and it was all she could do not to run the rest of the way and throw herself into his arms.

'*Buona sera*, Laura,' he said, smiling as he came forward. 'What an enchanting dress. You look more beautiful each time I see you.'

So do you, she thought fervently. 'Thank you. I'll just leave my key.' She pressed the bell and gave the key to Signora Rossi, who wished them both a pleasant evening.

Outside in the sunset light Domenico eyed her intently as they crossed the familiar bridge. 'What did you do today, Laura?'

'After I delivered the package to your hotel I walked to the Guggenheim,' she said in a tone that won her a wry look.

'You did not care for this?'

'It was interesting,' she said neutrally.

'Interesting,' he repeated, smiling a little as they strolled along the familiar route to the Piazza San Marco.

Laura described her tour of modern art and the switch to Renaissance architecture in the afternoon, but as they turned into the *piazza* she paused to look him in the eye. 'I didn't enjoy any of it, Domenico. After our disagreement last night I was miserable all day. I did those things just to kill time, which is a totally barbarous thing to do in a place like Venice.'

He seized her hand. 'I also was miserable—until this afternoon, when I received your gift.'

'I left it at the hotel fairly early this morning,' she informed him huskily.

'I did not return there until just before I rang you.' Domenico waved in acknowledgement to someone passing by, then began to walk faster. 'Come. We shall take a water taxi from the Molo.'

'Where are we going?'

'Before we dine I thought you might like a walk in the Giardini Pubblici. They are gardens in the quiet part of Castello.' He smiled down at her. 'Or are you worn out with so much walking today?'

'Not in the least,' she assured him, and returned the smile with such radiance his grasp on her hand tightened painfully.

The journey by water taxi was so brief Laura laughed at Domenico as he helped her out. 'We should have walked.'

'You must not return to your family exhausted, Laura!'

Far from tired, she felt like dancing along as she strolled with Domenico in tranquil, leafy gardens she had never expected to find in Venice.

'The pavilions here exhibit contemporary art at the Biennale, but this happens only on odd-numbered years,' he said, and grinned. 'So you are spared more modern art this evening, Laura.'

'Thank heavens for that. Though with you for company I would have enjoyed it—probably the Guggenheim and the churches as well,' she said honestly. 'But today nothing pleased me because I was alone and miserable.'

'Ah, Laura!' Domenico looked round swiftly, then bent to give her an urgent kiss. 'Even if I embarrass you in public I need this.'

Her eyes sparkled. 'Did I cause *you* any embarrassment by turning up at your hotel this morning?'

He shook his head, smiling. 'It was a great surprise to find that a Miss Laura Green had left a package for me, but I was delighted, not embarrassed.'

She slanted a look at him. 'I thought you might have been teased by the others on the staff, and brought me here by boat to avoid walking past the Forli Palace.'

He gave her a look of mock affront. 'My concern was for you alone.'

She laughed at him, and he stroked a caressing finger down her cheek. But as they resumed their leisurely stroll Laura's curiosity intensified as to what exactly Domenico did at his hotel. She longed to assure him that however menial his job she would still feel the same about him. But her relief at their reconciliation was so intense she kept quiet on the subject rather than risk spoiling their last evening together, and a few minutes later they were seated at a table on the canalside terrace of a restaurant renowned, Domenico told her, for its seafood.

'I hope you are not tired of fish?'

'Not in the least,' Laura assured him. 'Tell me what to choose.'

'They do a very good spaghetti dish here—*alla busana*, with scampi, tomato and chilli.'

'Sounds wonderful.'

Everything about the evening was so wonderful to Laura after the unhappiness of the day that the only shadow came when Domenico gave her a sombre look as they left.

'I wish so much that you were not leaving tomorrow, Laura.'

'So do I. But at least,' she added, determinedly cheerful, 'I shall have the memory of this evening to look back on when I'm slaving away in London.'

'Our evening has not ended yet, *cara*.'

'True. We have the walk back yet—'

'We shall return by boat,' he said promptly.

She shook her head. 'It's much too expensive to keep zipping about in water taxis.' Then it occurred to her that maybe he really didn't want to walk past his hotel.

'Let's go more slowly by *vaporetto* so I can take my last look at the lagoon by moonlight.'

It was a bittersweet experience to stand with Domenico at the rail for the last time. Laura gave a deep sigh when they left the boat. 'This time tomorrow I'll be home in Stavely.'

'I know,' he said sombrely, and took her hand. 'Ring me the minute you arrive, *per favore*.'

She nodded silently.

He looked down at her in question. 'It is much too early to take you to the hotel. Would you like some tea, Laura?'

Her heart leapt. 'Yes, please.'

'Will you come home with me to drink it?'

'Yes, please.'

He laughed softly. 'Such a polite English miss. Yet last night you stabbed me to the heart!'

'Such a dramatic Venetian *signore*,' she mocked.

'It is the truth,' he assured her. 'I did not sleep last night.'

'Because I was so horrible?'

'Yes. But also because I desired you so much my frustrated body would not let me rest.'

Laura flushed hectically, glad of the dim lighting as they

left the *piazza*. 'I had something of the same trouble,' she admitted gruffly.

He stopped dead. 'Are you saying you longed for me as much as I longed for you?' he demanded.

She nodded. 'That's never happened to me before.'

'Then you have not felt passion for the men in your life,' he said with satisfaction as they resumed walking.

'There haven't been *that* many,' she protested.

'Bene.' When they reached his apartment he took her hand to walk upstairs then unlocked his door and ushered her inside. 'But whatever their number in the past, Laura, it is now just one, yes?'

For answer she threw her arms round him as she'd wanted to the moment she'd seen him earlier, wanting but not quite daring to tell him that now he was the only man she wanted in her life. Ever.

Domenico's arms closed round her in possession, his cheek on her hair as they held each other in silence. After a while he released her and took her into the kitchen. 'You want tea,' he said unevenly.

'Actually, I don't. I said I did because I hoped you'd bring me back here,' she said candidly, and caught her breath at the brilliance of his smile.

'So what would you like, *carissima*?'

'I want to hold hands with you and just enjoy being together for the time we have left,' she said simply.

'Bene,' he said, stroking a hand down her cheek. 'Because that is almost exactly what I wish to do, also.'

'Almost?'

He shrugged. 'I cannot lie, Laura. I am a man, therefore I want more than just to hold hands.'

'You're honest!' she said as they went into the *salotto*.

The translucent eyes shadowed slightly. 'I try to be.' He took off his jacket and drew her down beside him. 'Laura, I would have rung you today, even without receiving your gift.'

'Really?'

'I could not have parted with you in such a way.'

'It would have made my flight home pretty miserable,' she admitted.

There was silence for a moment, then Domenico turned to her. 'It is madness to think that mere money should keep us from seeing each other.'

'It's a big thing to me, Domenico.' She leaned against his shoulder. 'I didn't have a holiday last year, so my mother gave me money for my birthday on condition I put it towards the villa-share I was offered in Tuscany. As I told you before, I earn a good salary, but I budget very carefully so I can save a bit for Abby and buy the reasonably smart clothes I need for my job. And I'd love to have my hair cut in one of those spiffy short styles, but keeping it long is cheaper so I don't.'

'Do not cut your beautiful hair, ever,' he said vehemently. 'Laura—'

'No, hear me out. I'm trying to explain why, much as I long to come back to Venice, I can't before next year at the very earliest, Domenico.'

He turned to stare at her in consternation. 'Next year!'

She nodded ruefully. 'But if you like travelling couldn't you come to London instead? Or don't you get enough time off from your job?'

'If it is the only way to see you I shall make time,' he assured her. 'Is there room for me in your flat?'

'Yes.' Laura looked at him squarely. 'But there's only one bed.'

Domenico drew in a deep, unsteady breath. 'I have tried,' he said roughly, 'but I am only human, *carissima*.' He lifted her onto his lap and kissed her with undisguised longing.

'*Amore,*' he whispered. 'I want you so much. Do you want me?'

She touched a hand to his cheek. 'Not just want. I couldn't sleep last night, afraid I'd never have the chance to tell you I'm very much in love with you, too, Domenico.'

This confession was too much for him. He kissed her fiercely, then scooped her up to carry her to the bedroom, which up to now had been unknown territory. But, utterly bowled over by being carried off in Domenico's arms, Laura had no eyes for décor as he laid her down on the bed. He stretched out beside her and held her close, his cheek against hers.

'You are trembling,' he whispered.

She nodded. 'You are, too.'

He gave a husky, muffled laugh. 'I know a cure for this.'

Laura wriggled closer. 'Cure me, then.'

'First,' he whispered, 'I must take down your hair.'

'Will that stop the shaking?'

'No, but it will give me very great pleasure!' When her hair streamed down in a gleaming cascade Domenico drew in a deep, relishing breath and threaded his fingers through it as he kissed her. Laura returned his kisses for a long, breathless interval, then pushed him away and stood at the side of the bed, shaking her hair back from her flushed face.

'I must go back to the hotel looking respectable, Domenico, so if only for practical reasons I'd better take my dress off.' She kicked off her shoes, then sat on the bed with her back to him. 'Would you undo my zip, please?'

'I like these practical reasons!' He sat up to plant kisses down her spine as he laid it bare, then stood up and drew her to her feet to smooth the dress from her shoulders. Laura stepped out of it and held it out to him, her colour high as his eyes moved over her with a possessive look as tactile as a caress. He laid the dress carefully over a chair, then snatched her up again and sat down with her on his lap to press kisses all over her face. When he raised his head she began to loosen his tie.

'Your turn now,' she said breathlessly.

'Be careful, *amore*,' he warned, in a tone that turned her to jelly, 'this tie is very special to me.'

Laura slid to her feet and handed it to him. 'You can put it away, then.'

Domenico took it to join her dress, and then in sudden impatience took his shirt over his head, kicked off his shoes and stripped down to silk boxers before picking her up again to lay her on the bed. He let himself down beside her and took her face in his hands. 'We are still shaking,' he pointed out.

Laura smiled into the luminous blue eyes. 'So what do we do to stop it?'

'First,' he whispered, 'I do this.' He undid her bra and tossed it away. 'Then I do this.' He paid loving, incendiary attention to each breast, his hands stroking and his lips on each nipple in turn with a delicate graze of teeth that sent such streaks of fire darting down inside she gasped and thrust her hips against him. He breathed in sharply, and moved his mouth lower over her ribs and down the slight swell of her stomach as he removed the last small lacy obstacle to kiss the mound beneath it. She stiffened, and pushed at his shoulders, and at once he slid back up her body, his eyes questioning.

'You do not like this?'

She shook her head, flushing. 'It's a mystery to me why a man should want to do that.'

Domenico laughed joyously. 'Ah, Laura. Has no man ever explained the mystery to you?'

'No. It's not a subject I care to discuss.'

'Discussion is a mistake. A practical demonstration is better—and you like things practical, yes?'

'I thought you were going to cure this shaky feeling, but

it's even worse now,' she accused, and with sudden impatience slid a hand over the black silk, grasping him through it in a caress that brought such a groan she released him in shock. 'Oh, Domenico, did I hurt you? I'm sorry!'

He closed his eyes tightly as he fought for control. Laura gazed up into his face and put her arms round him, hugging him close as he rubbed his cheek blindly over her hair.

At last Domenico let out an unsteady breath. 'This will be the first time we make love, also the last for much too long. I want it to be perfect for you, so do not touch me like that, *carissima* or this will not be possible. As I have told you before, I am not made of stone.'

It had felt frighteningly like it to Laura, a discovery that escalated the shaking problem still further as Domenico made love to her with skill and passion she responded to with ardour, which delighted him as he caressed her into a state of longing so intense that this time she yielded to the touch of his seeking lips and tongue in the place no man had ever kissed before. Shock waves of sensation surged through her entire body, rocketing her to climax as Domenico held her close, whispering ragged endearments in his own language.

When she was quiet in his arms, he smoothed her hair from her forehead and smiled down into her dazed eyes. 'Now you know why a man wishes to kiss and caress you that way, yes?'

'It was obvious what it did for me, but nothing happened for you, Domenico,' she said, frowning.

He smiled indulgently. 'It is a most wonderful thing for a man to know that he has given his woman such pleasure, *tesoro*! And when you are ready for me again I shall share the pleasure with you.'

His hands and lips and tongue caressed with such skill that soon Laura was on fire for him again and Domenico slid his hands into her hair, his eyes blazing in triumph as he moved between her thighs to enter her with slow, exquisite care, little by little, until at last she gave a ragged gasp of pleasure as he thrust deep inside her. She hugged him closer and he kissed her open mouth, murmuring in his own tongue as he began to move, gradually increasing the tempo as she moved with him until they reached a frenzied rhythm, which brought them to culmination so overwhelming they stayed joined, close in each other's arms long after it was over. ·

When Domenico raised the head he'd buried in Laura's hair his smile flipped her heart over. 'We are not shaking,' he observed huskily.

'No,' she agreed unevenly. 'You cured it.'

'We cured it together,' he corrected. 'Perfectly, beautifully together, *carissima*.'

She heaved a deep, unsteady sigh.

'Why do you sigh, Laura?' he asked, smoothing her hair from her forehead.

'I was just wishing I could stay here like this and not move until tomorrow morning,' she said frankly, and smiled sleepily as his arms tightened.

'I also,' he said, and kissed her gently. 'But Signora Rossi will expect me to bring you back by midnight, *Cenerentola*. I will come back for you early in the morning, and we shall have one last breakfast together before I take you to the airport.'

'But won't you be needed at your hotel?' she said anxiously.

'Not until I have taken you to Marco Polo.'

'You have a very accommodating job, Domenico!'

'I will tell you all about it in the morning,' he promised, and smiled down at her. 'Tomorrow we talk; tonight is for love.'

It was well past midnight when they reached the Locanda Verona, but Signora Rossi merely smiled indulgently when Domenico apologised for keeping her guest out a little later on her last night in Venice. He wished the *signora* goodnight, then turned to Laura and raised her hand very formally to his lips.

'Sleep well. I shall come for you in the morning.'

She gave him a demure smile and said, *'Grazie, e stata una magnifica serata.'*

The blue eyes narrowed wickedly. 'It was a wonderful evening for me, also.'

'Goodnight, Domenico.'

'Goodnight, Laura.'

When the door closed behind him Laura felt suddenly so tired she could hardly keep her eyes open. She received her key, asked for her bill to be made ready for the morning, wished the *signora* goodnight, and drifted up to her room in a happy daze. She managed to set her alarm before she fell into bed, and then slept like the dead until she woke to the ring tone of her phone next morning.

'Hello,' she said groggily, then shot upright at the sound of Domenico's voice.

'Laura! Are you awake?'

'I am now. Is something wrong?'

'Unfortunately, yes, *carissima*. There is a problem at the hotel. I have been called in to help with it—'

'And you can't come with me to the airport. Don't worry, Domenico. I'm sorry you can't make it, but I'll be fine.'

'I am more than just sorry,' he said urgently. 'There is so much I wish to say to you. Please ring me tonight.'

'I will,' she promised, keeping her voice steady by sheer force of will. 'Goodbye, Domenico.'

'Arrivederci, tesoro. Take great care, yes?'

'You too!'

Laura disconnected and dragged herself out of bed, so disappointed she wanted to howl. She'd so looked forward to travelling to Marco Polo with Domenico, greedy for every possible minute with him after the magic of their night. She sighed heavily, then pulled herself together and got on with her preparations for leaving. When she was showered, dressed, her suitcase packed and the room tidy, Laura went downstairs to pay the bill, which surprised her by being less than expected because, Signora Rossi explained, the room was on the attic floor, much smaller than the others and less popular due to the absence of an elevator, therefore there was a discount on the usual tariff. Laura thanked her warmly, received her passport, and after goodbyes set off for San Marco to catch the No. 1 Aligaluna boat to take the slow journey back along the Grand Canal to say her last, lingering goodbyes to Venice on her way to Marco Polo airport.

CHAPTER SIX

THE weather worsened over France. The descent into Heathrow was bumpy, and a very queasy Laura caught the train to Reading to get the next Intercity train to South Wales. Before she boarded it she rang her mother, who promptly volunteered to drive across the Severn Bridge to meet her. The train was packed and Laura escaped from it thankfully at Bristol Parkway, smiling broadly as she pulled her suitcase along the platform through the rain towards a small, hurrying figure in a dripping cagoule.

'Darling,' said Isabel Green, hugging her. 'Welcome home. How was Venice?'

'Fabulous. And a lot warmer than this. What a horrible day!' Laura kissed her mother warmly. 'You're a star for braving the bridge in this wind.'

'I thought you'd be glad to knock a bit off the journey and get home.'

They hurried through the rain to the car park and once Laura had stowed her belongings safely she sat back in the passenger seat with a sigh of relief. 'How's Abby?'

Isabel gave her daughter a triumphant little smile as they left the station. 'Working right now, but only to the end of the week, then she's off to France with Rachel Kent and her family. And after that she'll be able to play like all the other girls until she goes up to Cambridge.'

'How come?' Laura eyed her mother in astonishment. 'Have you won the lottery or something?'

'You're not far off. My Premium Bonds turned up trumps at long last. I won fifty thousand pounds!'

'*Really?* How absolutely wonderful!'

'When I got the cheque Abby and I did a war dance round the room!'

'I'm not surprised. Congratulations, you lucky old thing,' said Laura, laughing.

'Not so much of the old! What's in the parcel?'

'Candlesticks from Murano for Fen. I hope she likes them.'

'You can find out tonight. She'll be down later with your dress, and, I quote, demands to know every last thing you did in Venice.'

Laura flushed, glad her mother was concentrating too much on the road to notice. 'Trust Fen! Though she's entitled to a few details. Her brother-in-law sent someone to meet me from the airport. His name is Domenico and he took me out and about a bit while I was there.'

Isabel shot an amused glance at her daughter. 'Holiday romance?'

'He was just looking after me because Lorenzo Forli told him to.'

'Then you certainly got value for money. Was the hotel all right?'

'It was more boarding house than hotel, but spotlessly clean. My bedroom was tiny, but it had its own little bathroom and a fabulous view.' Laura chuckled. 'Now you're a lady of means you should try it yourself.'

'I may well do that some time.'

'You should. I helped myself to a brochure from the Locanda Verona as I left. Take Abby with you and overdose on culture together before she flies the nest.'

There was no more conversation for a while as they crossed the Severn Bridge. The speed limit was down to the minimum in the strengthening wind, which meant dogged concentration for Isabel as gusts buffeted the small car. She smiled at Laura in relief as she turned off for Chepstow.

'Thank heavens for that. Now, talk. Tell me more.'

Laura managed to keep Domenico out of it as much as

possible as she gave her mother a swift account of her stay in Venice, and then changed the subject. 'How are things coming along for the wedding of the year?'

Isabel smiled affectionately. 'Fenny's very calm about the whole thing. As long as she marries Joe Tregenna on the day she's not worried about anything else. But from a personal point of view I hope the weather relents by then. The label on my hat says, ''do not wear in rain''!'

When they turned off the main road up into Springfield Lane there was a pause in the proceedings. A herd of cows crossed from one field to another on the Morgan farm before Isabel could drive on through the narrow lane to Briar Cottage, which stood by itself half a mile from its nearest neighbour. When Isabel had first moved her daughters into it twelve years before the splendid view over the river had been no compensation to Laura for small rooms and a garden overgrown with brambles. It had been a painful contrast to the big Edwardian rectory she'd lived in all her short life until then. But because Isabel had crammed as many of their possessions as possible into it the three of them had soon come to look on Briar Cottage as home, and now, even with the rain lashing down like winter instead of summer, the rosy tint of the bricks glowed in welcome as they dashed up the path to the front door.

'Thank goodness,' gasped Laura as she came to a halt in the kitchen with her suitcase. 'I'll take this into the scullery and unpack my stuff straight into the washing machine, if that's OK. I need some of it to go back on Sunday night.'

'I'll make tea,' said Isabel, divesting herself of her cagoule. 'I bet you didn't have a decent cup all the time you were in Venice.'

Wrong, thought Laura, smiling at the memory of English Breakfast. 'After I've had a shower I'll drive into town to fetch Abby when she finishes, if you like.'

'No need. She's going straight from work to Rachel Kent's

party tonight and she's staying the night there afterwards. I said you wouldn't mind if she didn't dash home in between to see you.'

'Of course not. She deserves some fun. Fen will be down later, anyway.'

During the evening the conversation centred on Isabel's windfall and her plans for it, but when asked for more news of the holiday Laura changed the subject to the souvenirs she'd brought back. She wasn't ready, yet, to tell her mother more about Domenico. She needed to hear his voice first.

Isabel was delighted with her gifts, and put the crimson slippers on right away. 'They're much too good to wear round the house, but I'm going to, just the same. Thank you, darling. Tomorrow we'll find exactly the right place to hang this gorgeous mask. By the way,' she added, 'take Fenny up to your room when she comes. I shall be glued to my favourite murder serial.'

'Can't have you missing that,' agreed Laura, smiling.

A familiar screeching of tyres outside later heralded the arrival of Fenella Dysart. She shot up the path into the house, laid a sleeping bag on the kitchen table and hugged them both.

'Don't worry, Mrs G, I haven't come for a sleepover. The sleeping bag is keeping Laura's dress dry. Do you mind if I drag her upstairs to try it on?'

Isabel smiled affectionately. 'I was hoping you would, Fenny—my programme's about to start.'

'If it's the murder serial, Mother's glued to it as well!'

'Come on, then, Fen,' said Laura. 'Do you want coffee or a drink first?'

'Later, please. Let's take your ravishing creation up to your room and pray I haven't got any rain on it.'

Upstairs Laura hung the dress on her wardrobe door and eyed it closely. 'Looks good to me.'

'Get your kit off, then.'

Laura stripped off jeans and sweater, and held her arms up so Fen could lower the dress into place. Laura slid her feet into the satin shoes dyed to match and looked in the cheval mirror tucked into a corner. 'Nice!'

'Nice? It's perfect—and about as near the colour of your eyes as mere fabric can possibly be. Am I a genius, or what?'

The amber crêpe sheath fitted closely down to the knees, where three finely pleated, satin-bound tiers hung to just above the ankles. 'I had doubts,' admitted Laura, 'but it actually looks rather good. I could wear it with boots later on, maybe.'

'It's perfect,' said Fen with satisfaction. 'Let's go down and show your mother, then come back up here so you can tell me what Laura did in Venice.'

Once the dress was safely hung away, they both curled up with mugs of coffee at either end of the bedroom window-seat, which had been a favourite perch for both of them from the first day Laura had moved to Briar Cottage. All the way home on the plane Laura had been dying to tell her friend about the man who'd met her at the airport, but the moment she mentioned him Fen held up a hand.

'Didn't Giando meet you off the plane, then?' she said, frowning. 'I suppose he pushed the job onto someone else! I know Lorenzo told him to meet you, because Jess reported back to me.'

'A man called Domenico Chiesa came to meet me,' said Laura slowly.

'That's the one. I forgot he goes by Domenico these days. He's still Giando to the family, though.'

Laura eyed her with dawning suspicion. 'Is this the Giando I think it is?'

'You bet.' Fen thrust her dark hair behind her ears. 'He came to that language college in Cheltenham for a while when we were in school, but I don't think you actually met him. Gian Domenico Chiesa is Lorenzo's cousin. His mother's a Forli. His father used to run the Venice hotels, but he's retired now, so Giando—sorry, Domenico—is in charge. He's a busy bloke these days, so I'm glad he kept his promise and went to meet you.'

'He wasn't very happy about it,' said Laura, after a pause. 'He hustled me off to the *vaporetto* so quickly I felt like an utter nuisance.'

'Not his usual style,' said Fen, surprised. 'He's normally a wow with the girls. Anyway, was the hotel all right? Apparently Lorenzo emphasised that you were on a tight budget, and *very* prickly on the subject of favours.'

Laura's chin lifted. 'I prefer to call it independent. Anyway, the hotel was lovely, and only a short stroll from the Piazza San Marco. No food, though. I had to eat out.'

'So what did you do altogether?'

Once again Laura gave a list of restaurants and places visited as she took two parcels from the wardrobe. 'Here you are. The small one's a souvenir, so look at that first. The other one is your wedding present. I bought it in Murano. Not antique, but I hope you like it.'

Fen grinned as she took out a bright gold T-shirt with the Venezia logo. 'Been there, bought the T-shirt, I see. Thanks, Laurie—great colour. Now, what have we here?' Her eyes widened in delight as she took the candlesticks from their box. 'Oh, my goodness. They're absolutely beautiful!' She sniffed hard and hugged Laura tightly. 'Thanks a million. They'll be perfect on our new dining table—well, old table, really. I can't wait to show Joe.'

Laura smiled brightly. 'And where is Mr Tregenna right now?'

'In the bosom of his family in Cornwall this weekend.' Fen heaved a sigh. 'I've moved back home until the wedding, and it's going to be a long, long week. I miss Joe already.' She grinned suddenly. 'I know Miss Ice Maiden doesn't understand such things, but one day you'll meet someone you can't live without, too.'

With a sinking feeling that she'd done that already, Laura shrugged, smiling, and collected their coffee mugs. 'Mother's programme must be over now. She's dying to see the candlesticks—or *candeliere* as they say in Venice.'

'Show-off!' Fen looked at her watch. 'I'll just pop in to see Mrs G, then I must fly. I'll see you tomorrow night for the hen party—don't be late. Seven sharp up at the house before we paint Pennington red!'

After Fen left Laura went out to the kitchen—officially to check on her laundry, but in reality to seethe in silence over Domenico's silence about his relationship to the Forlis. Had Domenico been afraid she'd presume on it? No wonder he'd refused to take her to the Forli Palace to eat. The staff might have thought she was someone who mattered instead of just a holiday fling! Thank God she'd found out who he was before prattling on to Fen about shopping expeditions and candlelit dinners.

When Laura took two mugs of tea into the sitting room her mother looked up from the brochure of the Locanda Verona. 'Nice little place,' she commented.

'Very affordable, too. I was given a discount because my room was small and I had to climb four flights of stairs to get to it.'

Isabel frowned. 'It says here that there's a supplement on single rooms, no mention of a discount.'

Laura looked at the price tariff long and hard, then sprang to her feet, snatched her phone from her bag and punched a couple of buttons. 'Fenella Dysart, I want a word with you!'

'You just had one, bridesmaid. What's up?'

'Did you do some number-crunching regarding my hotel in Venice, by any chance?'

'I most certainly did not!' said Fen indignantly. 'Did they overcharge, or something?'

'Or something,' said Laura grimly. 'It was under, not over. I was given a hefty discount on my room—in summer, in Venice. And in San Marco at that.'

'Well, it's nothing to do with me, honest. I just asked Lorenzo to organise a nice place you could afford. Do you want to ring him in Florence and give *him* hell?'

'No, of course not.'

'Then look on the discount as a windfall—'

'Charity, you mean!'

'No, I don't, touchy! See you tomorrow.'

Isabel Green looked at her daughter's set face with foreboding. 'You think Lorenzo or maybe Jess paid the difference?'

'I'll ring Signora Rossi at the hotel before I make any wild accusations.'

'Take it easy, darling. You were charged less, not more.'

Laura took her phone upstairs to her room and eventually got through to the Locando Verona.

After the pleasantries were over Laura came straight to the point. 'Regarding my bill, Signora Rossi, I've just been looking at your hotel brochure, and there's a supplement on single rooms, but no mention of a discount. I'm sure I owe you money.'

There was a pause followed by an audible sigh. 'You owe me nothing, Miss Green. The difference in price has been paid.'

Laura stiffened. 'In that case, Signora Rossi, it's very important that you tell me who paid it, so I can thank them for such kindness. Was it Signor Lorenzo Forli, by any chance?'

'No, Miss Green, it was Signor Chiesa,' said the woman with reluctance.

'Ah. I see. Thank you so much for telling me. *Arrivederci.*'

Laura ground her teeth as she disconnected. Other people booked their holidays over the Internet, or went to travel agents, but her hotel reservation had come via Fen's brother-in-law, so it had never occurred to her to query it, even when she got a non-existent discount. But Domenico/Giando probably didn't think of it as charity. Her eyes narrowed ominously. Maybe he considered it fair exchange for their session in bed.

Laura went downstairs to reassure her mother that she didn't owe anything for her holiday after all. 'Lorenzo told one of his minions to sort it. I'll thank him at the wedding.'

Isabel smiled, relieved. 'How kind of him. Now, go to bed, darling, you look tired.'

Laura went upstairs, but not to bed. Instead she curled up on the window-seat, watching the rain stream down the glass. When her phone rang a long time later, as she'd known it would some time, she pressed the button and said a toneless hello.

'Laura, where have you been?' demanded Domenico frantically. 'You are safe? You did not ring—'

'Good evening, *Giando*!'

'Ah,' he said with a sigh, 'you have already spoken with Fenella.'

'Oh, yes. I've spoken with Signora Rossi, too. I asked her to explain the discount on my bill, and she told me you paid the difference.'

'So? I paid some of the charge. Is this so great a crime?'

'No, it's something I like far less—charity.'

'Cosa?'

'*Carita,*' she snapped, then let silence fall for a moment. 'Or maybe you just intended it as reimbursement.'

'*Dio*, this is so difficult on the telephone,' he said heatedly. 'What do you mean by reimbursement?'

'We made love, remember.'

'You think I have forgotten—?' He paused. 'Are you saying,' he demanded in sudden fury, 'that I paid this money in return for *that*? *Grazie!*'

'I'm the one who should be angry, Domenico. You were

so forthcoming with your other confessions, why didn't you just say who you were? Were you afraid I'd cash in on it if I knew you owned the hotel instead of just working there?'

'I do work in it,' he said harshly. 'And my reason for secrecy is simple. I was acting on orders from Lorenzo. He said you would resent special treatment.'

'A good thing he doesn't know just how special your treatment was!' she retorted.

There was silence for a moment. 'It was special to me,' said Domenico wearily. 'The so-practical Miss Green will find this hard to understand. After I spent time with you that first evening I kept my identity from you because I am a romantic fool. I wanted to be liked for myself for once, not because I am cousin to Lorenzo and Roberto, or because I am in charge of the Venice hotels in the Forli Group. I would have told you everything over breakfast this morning, but a guest at the hotel needed urgent medical attention and I do not delegate such matters to others.'

'I can understand that—'

'*Ottimo!* Then understand this, too, Laura. I thought of a way to pay part of your hotel bill because I cared for you and wished to ease your financial situation.' His voice hardened. 'But if obligation to me is so intolerable the remedy is simple—send me the money. *Arrivederci.*'

'Domenico—' But he'd disconnected before she could say a word. She waited for a minute, then rang him back, but he'd switched his phone off. And, she realised miserably, he'd used the past tense about caring for her.

When she felt able to talk about it without crying her eyes out Laura went to her mother's room to tell her the sad tale.

Isabel Green heard her out in silence. 'Darling,' she said gently at last, 'you really must learn to accept some things in the spirit they are given.'

'But not *money*, Mother!'

'But if you didn't know that Domenico paid it until now, it's obvious he didn't expect anything in return.'

'I know.'

'Then why all the drama?'

Laura raised wet eyes to her mother. 'Because I'm in love with him, or at least with the man I thought he was.'

'And what exactly did you think he was?'

'Someone who merely worked in a hotel—not owned the damn thing! It was obvious he wasn't short of money from his apartment and the way he dresses, but I assumed he had some management job, or whatever. If I'd known the truth I'd have kept my stupid mouth shut.'

'About what?'

'Domenico was so insistent that I go back to Venice soon, I had to explain why I couldn't. I gave him chapter and verse about keeping to a tight budget.'

'Did you include the bit about helping with Abby's college fund?'

'Oh, yes. The complete sob story.' Laura's mouth twisted in disgust. 'When I found he'd paid some of my bill I felt as though I'd been hinting for a handout.'

'Is he in love with you?'

'He said he was. But I doubt that he is any more. He's a typical Venetian male—proud as the devil, and takes offence easily.'

'You two have a lot in common, then,' said Isabel, lips twitching.

Laura stared at her mother, incensed, for a moment, but at last smiled reluctantly. 'Am I so bad, then?'

'Not bad—independent. You've had this bee in your bonnet about being the man of the house since you were ten years old.' Isabel patted her hand. 'Relax, darling. Things are different now. You don't need to help with Abby any more. Apart from my windfall, I'm still only forty-seven, remember. I can carry on teaching for quite a while yet.'

'I just wish you didn't have to.'

'But, darling, I love my job. What would I do with myself all day in this doll's house if I didn't work?'

Laura stared at her mother, taken aback. 'I never thought of it like that. I assumed you went back to teaching because you had to.'

'I did. But I'm fortunate, because it's a vocation for me, not just a job. It helped me through that terrible time after your father died, and because I was lucky enough to get a place at the village school I was always there for you and Abby—with a little help in the babysitting department from Grandma.'

The mention of her much-mourned grandmother was the last straw. Laura laid her head down on the bed, sobbing her heart out, and Isabel stroked her hair in silence until the storm had run its course.

'Sorry about that,' Laura said hoarsely as she got up at last.

Isabel looked troubled. 'If you really care for this man, can't you mend things between you?'

'I might have tried if he'd just been a hotel employee, but not now. Gian Domenico Chiesa is right out of my league. Don't worry. I'll just write off the experience as a holiday romance and forget about him.'

'Can you do that?' said her mother gently.

Laura shrugged. 'I'll have to. And in the meantime there's Fen's hen party to get through tomorrow night. That should chase the blues away!'

Abby backed into the room with a tray early next morning. 'Room service! Hi, sis. Welcome home. Sorry to wake you up, but I just dashed home for a clean apron. I'm off to work again in an hour.'

Laura heaved herself up, smiling at her sibling as she received the tray. In spite of working the day before and partying well into the night Abby looked as fresh as a daisy. 'Hello, love! Good party last night?'

'Brilliant! Ma's made your favourite scrambled eggs and soldiers, and orders you to eat it or else.'

'You shouldn't be waiting on me, Abby. You'll get enough of that the rest of the day.'

Abby grinned as she fastened her gleaming dark hair back with an outsize barrette. 'I gave in my notice yesterday. You heard about our amazing parent's stroke of luck? It means I can use my café money to go to France with the Kents, and Ma can go off on that holiday to the Lakes she fancies. And you can spend your spare cash on orgies instead of on me.'

'That'll be the day. By the way, I brought you something. Over there on the dressing table.'

Abby gave a squeal of delight and jumped up in a flurry of long, denim-clad legs. 'Was Venice as fabulous as it's supposed to be?' she demanded as she tore at wrappings.

'Even more so.'

Abby crowed as she pulled on a bright vermilion T-shirt emblazoned with 'Venezia' across the chest. 'I love it,' she said, eyeing herself in the mirror. 'Thanks a lot, Laurie. I'll wear it tonight.'

'Another party?'

'No, a sort of date.' Abby took out the coloured glass earrings and tried them on. 'How do I look?'

'Great. That colour's good on you. Who's the lucky man?'

'Just Marcus.'

'Rachel's brother?' Laura downed some of her tea to avoid mentioning that Marcus was a trainee barrister, and way out of her baby sister's league. 'Is he joining the family party in France?'

'No. But tonight he's got tickets for an open-air concert at Millwood House—picnic in the park, kind of thing. Mrs Kent's too busy getting ready for the hols, and Rachel can't stand classical music, so he asked me if I'd like to go along.'

'Then take a groundsheet and wear wellies. It was very wet last night.'

Abby turned a searching look on her sister. 'You look a bit peaky. Headache?'

'A bit,' admitted Laura, and grinned ruefully. 'I need to get rid of it, fast. Hen-party tonight.'

Laura caught the train back to Paddington the following afternoon, changed to the underground for Bow, and trudged up the stairs to her first-floor flat in a building that had been a match factory in a previous life. Her phone had remained obdurately silent all the way. Not that she had really expected to hear from Domenico, but she'd hoped. She frowned, still undecided whether to send the money to him or not. She'd thought about it endlessly, not sure whether he would take this as further insult to his pride, or whether it was appeasing her own. But the man had said 'send me the money', so he could hardly complain if she did.

Laura rang her mother to report in, assured her she was fine and promised to make herself some supper. She had tried hard to enjoy the roast Sunday lunch Isabel had prepared, but it had been an uphill struggle, which had not gone unnoticed. She smiled bleakly. Breaking up with Domenico was likely to be very good for her figure. She made some coffee, but instead of eating she ironed a white shirt, ready for next day, and when her phone rang felt shattered because her caller was Fen, not Domenico.

'Are you OK, Laura? You looked tired at the party last night.'

'Jet lag.'

'After a flight from Venice? Come off it. Anyway, in all the excitement I forgot to mention the wedding rehearsal. Can you make it back here for about six on Friday?'

'I'll take my stuff to work with me and leave early.'

'Great. You were such a star, doing the chauffeuring through all that rain last night. Thanks again, Laurie.'

'I take my role of chief bridesmaid very seriously!'

'And very well you do it. I couldn't make it on the big day without you.'

'Of course you could. All you really need is Joe waiting at the altar.'

'I know.' Fen cleared her throat. 'I'm so lucky. I wouldn't say this to anyone else, but I love him so much it hurts.'

Laura wouldn't have understood the hurt part before meeting Domenico, but she did now. 'Maybe you should tell Joe, too.'

'I have. I meant anyone other than you, Laura. Nothing horrible happened in Venice, did it?' asked Fen abruptly. 'You've been a bit fey since you got back.'

'It was a wonderful holiday.'

'Good. I was worried that Giando—sorry, Domenico—might have started you off on the wrong foot.'

'Not at all.' Laura paused, then shrugged and thought, Why not? 'Actually he called to see me to make sure I liked the hotel; even took me out to dinner.'

'*Now* you tell me?' Fen exploded. 'How did you get on together?'

'Very well, though he didn't mention at the time that he's related to Lorenzo, and runs the Venice end of the operation.'

'Why on earth not?'

'He wanted to be liked for himself, and not for his money and family connections.'

'With his looks? You've got to be kidding!'

'I think it's a hangover from the past—the lady who left him for his friend.'

'But that's years ago. And he must be over Alessa by now because Jess told me there's a new lady in his life.'

Laura stood very still. 'Really? Who is she?'

'Jess didn't have the details. But knowing Gian Domenico she'll be a knockout in the looks department, and decked out down to her knickers in Versace. You can ask him about her yourself on Saturday. He's coming to the wedding!'

CHAPTER SEVEN

JEALOUSY hit Laura like a tsunami. She spent the night cursing the day she'd met Domenico and bought the euros next morning. But just posting them wasn't enough. She wanted the satisfaction of handing them over in person—whether he had the new lady in tow at the wedding or not.

Having made the decision, Laura gave the souvenir earrings to her colleagues, Claire and Ellie, made them envious with tales of her holiday, and did her best to put Venice—and Domenico—from her mind. She was successful during the day because her work at a Docklands investment bank demanded her full attention. The job combined her regularly updated secretarial skills with her love of research, and Laura enjoyed gathering information from the Internet and institutions like Reuters, and the subsequent collation of reports; even the sorties into the frenzy of the trading floor afterwards to deliver them.

Evenings were occupied with friends from the bank for a drink and a snack after work, or with a swim in her building's pool and a workout in the gym. The infuriatingly restless nights were the worst problem. Laura ground her teeth as she tossed and turned into the small hours. If insomnia was a side effect of having a lover, she was glad she'd never had one before. Not that she'd ever had Domenico in the first place, of course. He probably used the same routine with every woman he sweet-talked into bed.

When Abby rang to say goodbye before she went off to France, Isabel took over the phone to announce that she'd booked a fortnight's holiday in the Lake District with her colleague and friend, Janet Fenton.

'Picturesque hotel, good food, and lots of walking to burn it off,' said Isabel. 'By the way, Fen tells me that your Domenico's coming to the wedding.'

'He's not mine, Mother.'

'He hasn't rung, then?'

'No. So you and Janet take care in the Lakes, Mother. Steer clear of holiday romances.'

'Chance would be a fine thing!'

Sleep caught up with Laura when she least wanted it, and to her fury she slept late on the Thursday morning. She shot out of bed, threw on her clothes, and with no time for coffee raced to the station, trod on a loose paving stone and fell flat on her face with such a smack she saw stars when she finally managed to sit upright. Shaken and hideously embarrassed, she sat very still on the kerb for a moment, checking that her teeth were intact. When her head stopped spinning she staggered up to collect the scattered contents of her handbag and almost fell again as pain shot through her ankle. Breathing heavily, she put her weight on her good foot as she leaned against a lamp post to rummage for tissues to mop up the blood pouring down her face.

'I say, are you all right?' said a voice, and Laura looked round to see a young man in a City suit peering at her. 'I saw you fall. Hellish tumble. Can I help?'

'That's very kind of you. If you can see my phone anywhere I'll call a taxi and get myself to a hospital,' said Laura shakily.

Her good Samaritan found the phone in the gutter and broke the bad news that it was broken. He used his own to ring for a taxi, then handed it over so Laura could contact her work, and afterwards, to her surprise, even insisted on waiting with her until it arrived. Laura thanked him warmly as he helped her into the cab, grateful for his help.

The A & E department was packed. Laura hobbled to

Reception to check in, then took a seat to wait until she was
assessed by a triage nurse who warned of a three-hour wait
to see a doctor. By the time Laura was finally examined she
had a pounding headache, her ankle was throbbing violently
and she could barely see over the swelling below her left
eye. But to her relief no fractures showed up on the X-rays
the doctor ordered. Her skull and face were intact, her ankle
was neither broken nor sprained, only badly wrenched, and
when it was bound up she was given painkillers and pronounced free to go. Laura rang for a taxi from the public
telephone and, desperate for fresh air, went outside, shoeless,
to sink down on a bench to wait, then stiffened in dismay
when she saw a familiar white-coated figure approaching, fair
hair ruffled, boyish face frowning in concern.

'Laura?' said Dr Edward Lassiter. 'Good God! What the
hell happened to you? Were you mugged? Has someone seen
you?'

'Hello, Edward,' she said coolly. 'I had a fall on my way
to work. I've just been X-rayed, but I didn't break anything.
I didn't know you'd transferred.' Or she would have gone to
another hospital.

'Started here last week.' He looked at his watch. 'I'm on
duty, otherwise I'd drive you home.'

'No need. I've rung for a taxi. It should be here any minute.'

He took her hand. 'Look, I've got to go, but I'll call round
to see you later—'

'Thank you, but I won't be there. I'm going home to
Stavely.' Laura detached her hand as a taxi drew up and with
a feeling of escape let him help her into it, knowing from the
look on his face that she'd offended Edward again, but feeling too ill to worry about it.

When she got in she took a long look in the bathroom
mirror and faced facts. She was a total mess. An ugly scab
bisected her eyebrow, one side of her swollen face was

grazed from half-shut eye to sore chin, and due to the ankle and various other contact points on her body she ached all over. But none of it mattered. The major tragedy was not only missing her best friend's wedding, but the chance of seeing Domenico again. Tears poured down her face at the thought, but they stung her grazed cheek so badly she mopped them up, took several deep breaths and left a message on her mother's phone to ask for a lift from the station a day sooner than planned, and warned that her mobile was broken.

Laura packed her bag, made some tea, took some pain-killers, and, after an interval with her foot up and a bag of frozen peas clamped to her face, put on dark glasses and a pair of elderly flat shoes, tied a scarf over her head to hide as much of her face as possible and went out to catch a train on the first leg of her journey home. And on the slow, painful way to the Bow Road station she steeled herself to ring Fen to report the fall.

In response to a frantic fusillade of questions Laura gave Fen the details, and eventually, after much argument, managed to convince her she would be one bridesmaid short. 'I'm so *sorry*, Fen,' she said miserably. 'I could kick myself.'

'For heaven's sake, don't! You're in enough trouble without that, by the sound of it. I'll pop down tonight to see you.'

Hours later Laura gave a sigh of relief when she saw her mother waiting for her on the platform at Bristol Parkway.

'Thank goodness you got my message,' she said gratefully, and took off the scarf and glasses. 'I had a fall this morning. Don't faint. It's not as bad as it looks.'

After frantic questions, and Laura's assurances that the requisite medical care had been taken, Isabel drove her daughter home. 'Bed,' she said firmly when they arrived. 'I'll bring your things in. Just get yourself upstairs and undress, darling.'

'Thank you,' said Laura gratefully. She crawled up the

steep stairs and sat down on the edge of the bed, feeling too wretched to undress. 'I feel a bit shaky,' she admitted when her mother came in with her holdall.

'I'm not surprised,' said Isabel as she piled pillows. 'You should have let me drive to the flat to fetch you.'

'I couldn't subject you to a journey to London and back on top of your working day!'

'I would have managed, and it would have been a lot better for you than hobbling around on the underground in that state. Why on earth didn't you get a taxi to Paddington?'

'Low on cash. Don't scold!'

Isabel put an arm round her contritely. 'Sorry, darling. Now, totter to the bathroom for a wash while I make some tea.'

In bed later, leaning back against cool pillows, her ankle propped up on another, Laura felt a little better by the time her mother arrived with a steaming beaker and a bag of ice.

'Are you sure you're not concussed?' Isabel demanded.

'Quite sure. They told me what to watch out for at the hospital.' Laura smiled ruefully. 'And to make my day I ran into Edward. He's just transferred there.'

'No! How did that go?'

'He wanted to come round to the flat tonight to check on me. I said no and offended him again.'

'Never mind Edward. Drink the tea, then lie back with that ice on your face.'

Fen came rushing up the stairs a few minutes later. She exclaimed in horror when she saw Laura's face, and sat down on the edge of the bed. 'Just look at you!' she said, appalled. 'Are you *sure* you haven't broken any bones?'

'The X-rays said not.'

'Thank heavens for that, at least.' Fen let out an explosive sigh. 'I was hoping that a few layers of slap would do the trick, Laurie.'

'I wish! You know I'd give anything to be at your wedding, but I'll just have to be there in spirit. The face would freak out the guests even without the limp.' Laura tried hard for flippancy, but Fen wasn't deceived.

'You feel rotten, poor love, don't you?'

'I'll live. Is everything going smoothly up at Friars Wood?'

'Now the family's started arriving it's a madhouse up there! I'm thinking of camping out in the marquee.' Fen leaned down and very carefully kissed Laura's uninjured cheek. 'I'll ring in the morning, but I'll go now before your mother comes to throw me out. Put the ice back on that eye and concentrate on getting better.'

Laura shrugged. 'No choice—back to work on Monday.'

'Stuff that!' snorted Fen.

Isabel brought up a tray later, and settled on the window-seat to make sure Laura ate the poached egg she'd agreed to.

'Term finishes at twelve tomorrow,' she said. 'I'll come home to see how you are, then go back to finish up with the rest of the staff.'

'No need for that. I'll be fine on my own. It's my face that's hurt—the rest is in reasonable working order.'

Isabel looked unconvinced. 'You need rest, my girl. I don't suppose you can read with that eye, and television's out right now, but I've got a new audio book from the library. It's a really gruesome thriller—you'll like it.'

Next morning Laura sat up in bed gingerly, decided she felt halfway human again, and limped downstairs before her mother could toil upstairs with her breakfast.

'What on earth are you doing up at this hour?' demanded Isabel.

'Making sure you don't run about waiting on me before you take off to school.' Laura pulled a face. 'I had a look in the mirror. The bruises are right down my neck now.'

'You took quite a crack on your chin, too,' said her mother, getting up to examine it. 'How's the ankle?'

'Bearable. A couple of painkillers and a few more cups of tea will help.'

Fen rang during the morning with anxious enquiries and messages of sympathy from every member of the Dysart family.

'Thank them for me,' said Laura, touched. 'Now go! Get on with being a bride, Fenella Dysart. Tomorrow is your big day, so concentrate on it and be happy.'

'I'll see you when we come back from Italy—we'll have a little party!'

Time hung so heavy Laura was very glad of company by the time her mother came home from school that afternoon. But it took effort to be cheerful during the evening, knowing that both of them should have been at the pre-wedding family dinner up at Friars Wood.

'There's no reason why you couldn't have gone, Mother,' said Laura, but Isabel shook her head firmly.

'Not without you, darling.'

Laura groaned in frustration. 'It's not fair that you should have to miss the fun, too.'

The wedding day dawned hot and sunny, but after an early call to the bride to wish her joy the morning was hard for Laura. It hurt to know she should have been up at Friars Wood in the thick of the Dysarts, having her face and hair done and helping with the trio of teenage bridesmaids, but, most important of all, just being there for Fen on her big day.

When Isabel came downstairs after lunch, the perfect wedding guest in a slim fawn linen dress and dashing bronze hat, she struck an exaggerated pose.

'How do I look?'

'Absolutely gorgeous! Off you go, or you won't find a place to park. Take lots of photographs, and give Fen a big kiss for me.' Laura hurried her mother to the door before either of them could get emotional, waved her out of sight, then with a sigh limped back inside to get through the long afternoon as best she could.

To kill time she washed her hair for the first time since the accident, but with a hair-dryer ruled out styling had to be restricted to gentle towelling and a very careful brush through. Afterwards Laura smoothed moisturiser into her skin, pleased that repeated applications of ice had at least reduced the swelling on the eye surrounded with arresting shades of maroon and plum. Making a face at it, she took wings of hair back from her ears, secured them on the crown of her head with a giant clip and let the rest hang down the back of her pink vest top to dry in the sun.

The garden went back a long way behind the house. In the years since the move Isabel had gradually transformed the bramble-choked wilderness into a haven of green lawn surrounded by flowering shrubs, which softened the outlines of the high laurel boundary hedges. A shallow rockery planted with alpines separated the lawn from the small, paved area outside the sitting room window, and during the morning Isabel had unfolded two director's chairs, and put up the parasol over the picnic table there for an early salad lunch.

All morning Laura had maintained such a determinedly cheerful mood it was a relief to relax now she was alone. She found an extension lead to attach to her tape-player, filled a jug with orange juice and ice cubes, collected a glass and went outside to sit under the parasol. She propped her feet up on a stool, and, eyes closed, listened to the church bells welcoming the guests arriving to see the youngest Dysart daughter married. Her mouth tightened as she wondered if one wedding guest in particular had arrived—and if he'd come with company. Laura thrust the thought away, and when the bells stopped sent a silent message of love to the bride, switched on the tape, and concentrated fiercely until the plot absorbed her again.

She leaned back, bare legs outstretched, removed the barrette and combed her fingers through her damp hair, and then sat utterly still other than to change the tape at intervals and refill her glass. She grew so drowsy in the afternoon warmth as the hours passed that when the current tape ended she couldn't be bothered to put in a new one.

Laura woke with a start from a restless doze and shot upright with a gasp of fright, her heart thumping madly at the sight of Domenico gazing down at her. Shaken and breathless, she shook the hair back from her incredulous face to meet blue eyes blazing with such horror she shut her own in self-defence. When she opened them again his familiar smile was firmly in place. A white gardenia adorned the lapel of a suit with the superb fit of all Domenico's clothes, and Laura was immediately, resentfully conscious of her battered face and untidy hair, her short denim skirt long past its shelf-life, and the crowning touch of scruffy old trainers loose enough for her swollen foot.

'*Come esta*, Laura,' Domenico said gently.

She pulled herself together, trying to breathe normally. 'Not at my best, I'm afraid,' she said unevenly, and thrust her hair behind her ears to display the full effect of her bruises. 'This is a surprise.'

He drew the other chair close and with a familiar '*Permesso?*' sat down. 'Ah, Laura!' His voice was husky with compassion as his eyes travelled over her face. 'Your mother told me of your fall, but I did not imagine—'

'That I looked so scary?'

'That you had been hurt so very badly,' he contradicted. 'Are you in pain still?'

'Not pain, exactly. My face is just sore and throbs a bit. So does my ankle.' She smiled coldly. 'If I'd expected to frighten anyone I would have worn a mask. I bought one in Venice, remember.'

'I do remember. And you did not frighten me,' he assured her. 'I feel only sympathy for your injury.'

She found that hard to swallow. 'The worst part was missing Fen's wedding. How did it go?'

'It was very beautiful. But to my great disappointment you were not in the bridal party.'

'You can see why now.' She smiled politely. 'It's very kind of you to take time to visit me, but shouldn't you be up at Friars Wood with the other guests?'

He shook his head. 'I have been there already. I congratulated the radiant bride and her proud husband, and introduced myself to your mother.' Domenico smiled warmly. 'She is so much like you. I recognised her immediately.'

'She looks good, doesn't she?' said Laura, thawing slightly.

'*Molto elegante,*' he agreed, and eyed her warily. 'Mrs Dysart consulted with your mother and made a suggestion.'

Laura raised her good eyebrow. 'What is it?'

'She gave me champagne so that you and I may toast the bride and groom together.' He smiled. 'The bride thought this was an excellent idea.'

'Did you come to the wedding alone, then?'

'Yes, of course,' he said, surprised. 'I have rung you twice since Thursday to say I was arriving today, but your number was unobtainable.'

'I broke my phone when I fell.' She eyed him suspiciously. 'Domenico, are you here because you feel sorry for me?'

'No.' His chin lifted. 'But if you do not want me here I will leave the champagne and go.'

She turned her face away, fighting sudden tears, but after a moment she was pulled to her feet and into Domenico's arms with her good cheek pressed to his crisp shirtfront.

'You took off your jacket,' she muttered, breathing in the

male scent that was so bone-meltingly familiar she almost forgot she was furious with him.

'My suit is new,' he explained. 'The shirt will wash.'

'And I thought I was the practical one!' She tried a laugh, which sounded so much more like a sob his arms tightened.

'Piangi!' he commanded, but having been told to cry Laura lost all desire to, and pushed him away.

'Sorry. My emotions are a bit near the surface since the fall.'

He winced, and touched a finger to her uninjured cheek. 'You could have done yourself such serious injury, Laura.' He paused. 'So. Shall I stay?'

She lifted a shoulder. 'If you like.'

'Then I shall fetch the champagne from the car.'

'I'll get some glasses.' Laura limped into the house, and for pride's sake took time to tie her hair back before collecting a couple of champagne flutes.

'I feel happier with my hair under control,' she told Domenico as she rejoined him.

He smiled a little. *'Bene.* I like you to feel happy.'

She raised a cynical eyebrow. 'Really? You were pretty cutting on the phone!'

Heat flared in his eyes. 'You hurt me so much, Laura.'

'You or your pride?' she said, unmoved.

He shrugged. 'Both. To help you I paid a very little part of your hotel bill, and in return you accuse me of paying for your body. I believed we had made beautiful love together,' he added angrily. 'So, yes, my pride was hurt.'

Her eyes flashed. 'So was mine, Domenico, when I found out you'd been having a little joke with me.'

'I have given you my reasons for that,' he reminded her, and without spilling a drop removed the cork from the champagne, filled two glasses and handed one of them to her. 'Now we make the toast,' he said.

'To Fen and Joe,' said Laura, raising her glass.

'To the bride and groom,' he agreed, and raised his own. 'Also a toast to you, Laura, with the wish that your beautiful face will soon be whole again.'

'I'll drink to that!' she said dryly. 'Though even at its best my face is hardly beautiful.'

'It is to me,' he said softly.

But Laura couldn't forget Domenico's knee-jerk reaction at first sight of it, nor the lady back in Venice somewhere. 'It was kind of you to come,' she said politely. 'I was feeling pretty blue earlier on.'

'It is very sad that you could not be at your friend's wedding,' he agreed. 'When I learned that you were hurt I wanted to come here at once to see you. But I had to wait while many photographs were taken, then drive to the Dysart home to congratulate the bride and groom, also to ask your mother her permission to visit you.' Domenico smiled. 'She is a charming lady.'

'That she is,' agreed Laura. 'Where are you staying?'

'At an inn called the Forrester's Arms. You know it?'

'Yes, it's a nice country pub with good food, but a far cry from the Forli Palace.'

'*Non importa.* A change is good, yes?'

'It will certainly be that—' She broke off as the phone rang, and excused herself to go inside to answer it. 'Hi, Mother.'

'Are you all right, darling?' asked Isabel anxiously.

'I'm fine.'

'Is Domenico still with you?'

'Yes.'

'How long is he staying?'

'I don't know. Are you ready to come home, then?'

'Actually, Frances wants me to stay on for a while, so if you've still got company maybe I will.'

'Stay as long as you like. Have fun. I'll see you later.' Laura put the phone down and went back to Domenico. 'That was my mother, asking how long you're likely to stay.' She smiled coolly. 'But you can go now, if you like. I'll be fine on my own until she comes home.'

His face darkened. 'You wish me to go?'

'Not quite yet. First there are one or two things I want to say. As you said, it's difficult over the phone—' She broke off as rain began to fall and reached for the tape-player. 'Grab your jacket and leave the rest. We'd better go inside.'

In the small sitting room Laura switched on lamps, waved Domenico to a chair and sat down on the sofa with her feet up.

'So tell me these one or two things,' he commanded, tearing his eyes from the length of bare brown leg on display.

'First,' began Laura, 'when we became lovers I didn't know who, or what, you were.'

He frowned. 'What do you mean?'

'It was obvious from your apartment and your clothes that you earned good money, but I took it you were in some management job at the hotel. I had no idea that you owned it.'

'I do not own it. The hotel belongs to the Forli Group, of which I am a part because I am family,' he said, with the air of one explaining to a child. 'I am in charge in Venice now because my father has retired.' He threw out his expressive hands. 'What difference does this make?'

'Quite a lot to me. You live among the pillars and frescoes of the Palazzo Forli or in your smart San Marco apartment overlooking the Grand Canal.' She waved a hand at the small, crowded room. 'I live here, or in my tiny flat in London.'

'So? I do not understand the problem.'

Her chin went up. 'It's not a problem any more. When we parted that last night I was moonstruck enough to think that a relationship of some kind was possible. But now I know the facts it's out of the question. You lied to me, Domenico.'

He sighed impatiently. 'I did not lie, exactly. It was so good to be with someone who seemed to like me for myself, I did not tell you—'

'That's not the lie I'm talking about. You said there was no woman in your life, yet according to Fen's sister, Jess Forli, there is.' Laura's eyes stabbed his accusingly. 'Admit it, Domenico, you said all that nonsense about falling in love just to get me into bed. And like a fool I fell for it.'

The translucent eyes narrowed to glittering shards of ice. 'There is no other woman in my life. And I did not lie about my feelings for you.' He got slowly to his feet and picked up his jacket, controlled fury in every move. 'But if you can believe such things of me you are right, Laura. There is no possibility of a relationship between us.'

'So why did you come here today?'

He smiled scornfully. 'Do not imagine it was to discuss this boring subject of relationships. My visit is courtesy only, because you are injured.'

'How very kind of you,' she managed, when she could trust her voice.

He put on his jacket, suddenly a remote, elegant stranger. '*Allora*, I must go back to the Dysart home to wish the bride and groom well before they leave for their honeymoon.'

Laura led the way into the hall to open the front door. 'Goodbye, then. Thank you for taking time to visit me.'

'*Prego,*' he said, shrugging.

'Wait—I almost forgot. I have something for you.' She went back into the sitting room to search in her handbag, then returned to him, holding out an envelope.

Domenico opened it, his face stony as he saw money. '*Grazie,*' he said savagely, and thrust the envelope in his pocket. 'Now you owe me nothing and you can be happy, yes? But tell me, Laura, if you had such harsh things to say, why did you not accuse me of these things at once and send me away?'

She smiled at him sweetly. 'I was bored. Your company was better than none.'

His eyes glittered with outrage for an instant, then with a graceful, insolent bow he strode off through the rain to his hired car. An Italian model, Laura noted dully. Domenico liked to maintain his image at all times and in all places.

CHAPTER EIGHT

LAURA rescued the champagne flutes, washed them and put them away, emptied the leftover wine down the kitchen sink, took some rubber boots and an umbrella from the closet, then, knowing her mother wouldn't be long, sat slumped at the table in a cagoule to wait. When she heard the car she limped down the path as fast as she could and managed to reach it just as Isabel switched off the ignition.

'Mother, put these boots on and leave your shoes in the car with your hat,' ordered Laura. 'You take the umbrella; I've got my hood up.'

Isabel followed her into the kitchen soon afterwards and thrust the dripping umbrella into the sink. 'Why did Domenico leave?'

'To speed the bride and groom on their way.'

'He could have stayed with you a lot longer. The happy couple are dancing the night away in the marquee with everyone else. Fenny won't leave until the band does.'

'Of course she won't. They're going back to Joe's house tonight. The real travelling starts tomorrow.' Laura smiled bleakly. 'Domenico was just making an excuse to get away, Mother.'

'From you?'

'Right.'

'You had a quarrel?'

'Not exactly. I just cleared the air a bit.'

Isabel dispensed with the boots and sat down at the table, motioning Laura to do the same. 'I like Domenico.'

'He likes you, too.'

'He was appalled when I told him what had happened to you.'

Laura glowered. 'Even more so when he actually laid eyes on my face!'

'Ah. I see,' said Isabel, enlightened.

'I was dozing in the garden, and he woke me up. But the Prince lost the plot. He stared at Sleeping Beauty in horror instead of kissing her awake.' Laura shrugged. 'Only for a split second, but long enough.'

Her mother sighed. 'So you sent him packing?'

'Not right away. He'd brought champagne to toast Fen and Joe, and I was tired of my own company by that time, so we sat in the garden until the rain started.'

'What went wrong?'

'I told him a relationship between us wasn't possible due to the difference in our circumstances—'

'What?'

Laura quailed at the look her mother gave her. 'Well, it isn't, is it?' she said defensively. 'You should see his apartment, not to mention the Forli Palace—'

'Stop right there. I've never heard such rubbish!' Isabel jumped up to fill the kettle. 'It's an insult to your father and me to say you're not good enough for Domenico Chiesa—or any other man, for that matter.'

Laura stared at her mother in dismay. 'I didn't mean it like that!'

'Then how did you mean it? This is the twenty-first century, Laura Green—do you want some tea?'

'No, thanks.'

Isabel sat down at the table again, a relentless look in her eye. 'Once you hit your teens you got this bee in your bonnet about charity. But I had no idea you felt inferior to people who possessed more in life than we do. Was that your reaction when Frances Dysart gave you generous presents for your birthday, or included you in outings with Fenny?'

'No!' said Laura, horrified. 'I don't mean that at all. The Dysarts always seemed like family to me.' She took a deep breath. 'My school uniform was the start of it.'

'Ah!' Isabel slumped slightly in her chair. 'The second-hand clothes from the school shop. They were a godsend to my bank balance. You never said you resented them, Laura.'

'Because I knew it was a struggle for you to send me to the same school as Fen. But I loathed having clothes that someone else had worn first.'

'Abby didn't feel like that,' said Isabel dryly. 'She loved wearing your cast-offs, until she grew too tall.'

'Ah, but my baby sister was not only clever enough to get a scholarship which paid her fees, she's also blessed with a better nature than me.'

'Different, not better.'

Laura frowned. 'If school fees were a problem, how did you manage to send me on school trips to France and so on?'

'Grandma paid. And if she were still with us she'd give you short shrift if you accused *her* of charity.'

'I wouldn't dare! But I wish I had known. I could have shown her I was grateful.'

Isabel shook her head in despair. 'She did it to give you pleasure, not to get gratitude.'

'Sorry!'

Isabel eyed her quizzically. 'So let me just get this straight. You fell in love with a man you thought had an ordinary job, even though he lives in an expensive apartment, wears wonderful clothes—if his suit today was anything to go by—and takes you out to pricey meals?'

'I insisted on paying for one of them!'

'Of course you did,' said her mother, resigned. 'Anyway, now that Domenico's revealed in his true colours, i.e. not just good-looking and charming but seriously well off, you're no longer in love with him. Am I right so far?'

'You make me sound like a complete fool, Mother. Which

I am, of course, because I'm still hopelessly in love with him,' said Laura miserably.

'But because he was horrified at the sight of your face you told him to get lost.'

'I had to get in first, in case he meant to dump *me*. You must have noticed that Domenico's pretty hot on appearances! But a relationship isn't possible between us anyway, because he'd lied to me.'

'About his identity?'

'Worse than that. In Venice he told me there was no woman in his life, and that he was in love with me. Otherwise I wouldn't have—have got so involved,' said Laura, flushing.

'And is there some woman in his life?'

'He says not, but Jess told Fen there is. So someone's wrong somewhere.'

'You didn't tell me about this.'

'I wanted to talk to Domenico first.'

'And he denied it. Then what?'

'He was pretty angry by that stage—'

'You surprise me,' said Isabel dryly.

'He did the arrogant Venetian thing, and looked down his nose as he informed me that he had not come for boring discussion of our relationship, but out of courtesy because of my fall.'

'Ouch! So what did you say to that?'

'Not a lot. I just gave him the money he'd paid Signora Rossi.'

Isabel groaned.

'At which point he said *grazie* and left. So that's that,' said Laura, and jumped to her feet. 'Maybe I will have some tea after all, while you tell me all about the wedding. I bet Fen looked amazing,' she added wistfully.

'She certainly did. Only someone with Fenny's lack of hips could carry off such a narrow column of satin. The girls looked a picture, and Frances had the most ravishing hat—'

Laura listened with determined attention while her mother described the clothes at the wedding, but got up when Isabel began to yawn. 'Bed,' she said firmly. 'You can tell me the rest tomorrow, before I go back to London.'

'*Tomorrow!* Look, darling, I can easily postpone my holiday for a while—'

'Absolutely not. You go off to the Lakes with Janet, and by the time I see you again I'll look less like an extra from a horror film.'

Laura kept to her plan, but with a lot less enthusiasm for the idea than she'd let on to her mother. And during her call home to report in when she got to the flat she was given the finishing touch to her day.

'Domenico called here after I drove back from the station,' said Isabel. 'He was not at all pleased to hear you're going back to work tomorrow.'

'It's not up to him to be pleased or not! What did he want?'

'To see you, I imagine. We chatted for a while, then he went off to a dinner Jess and Lorenzo were giving for the family at the Chesterton, and I got on with my packing.'

'Are you all set for the morning?'

'Yes. I'm picking Janet up at nine.'

'Then have a good time, both of you.' Laura stifled a yawn. 'Sorry. I need an early night. I'll give you my number as soon as I get a new phone. Until then ring me here at the flat. And drive carefully.'

'I always do. Take care of yourself, darling. If it's too much for you in work tomorrow, take more time off.'

'Yes, Mother.'

Laura had been fully prepared for loud exclamations about her appearance next day, not least because she was wearing tennis shoes with her black suit. The surprise was a lack of energy that affected her concentration. And the glasses she wore for computer work hurt her bruised face so much that by the end of the afternoon she was heartily glad to go home. She checked her mailbox in the lobby as usual, and found a parcel signed for by the concierge. Surprised, she took the lift to the first floor and tore the wrappings from a box that contained a mobile phone and a note.

This is not charity, Laura. It is a practical gift to wish you a swift recovery. Domenico.

Laura took out the pretty little object, smiling when she saw it came complete with all the latest bells and whistles. The gift was so obviously an olive branch she would be a fool to refuse it.

She rang Domenico before she could change her mind. 'This is Laura.'

'*Come esta?* You have just returned from your bank?'

'Yes.'

'Should you be working again so soon?'

'Probably not. It was a very tiring day.' Laura braced herself. 'But it was a very pleasant surprise to find your gift when I got home. Thank you very much.'

There was a lengthy pause. 'You are going to accept it?' he said at last.

'Yes, Domenico, I am.' She paused, then told him the truth. 'I thought it might alienate you completely if I sent it back. And I'd like to think we could at least be friends.'

'I would like that very much,' he said promptly. 'So. When I am in London you will dine with me?'

'Yes. I'll even let you pay for my dinner!'

'Then we make progress.' He paused. 'How is your face, Laura?'

She took a look in the mirror over the sink unit. 'It's starting to heal. I should be back to normal soon.'

'*Bene.* Are you very tired?'

'Not really.' Which was true now she was talking to Domenico again. 'It was kind of you to send the phone.'

'I expected it back by the next post.'

'Postage to Venice is far too expensive!'

He laughed. 'Always the practical one.'

'That's me. Thank you again. Goodbye, Domenico.'

'*Ciao*, Laura.'

Feeling a whole lot better, Laura stood in the shower for a while, careful to keep her hair dry rather than risk going to bed with it wet. She massaged more analgesic cream into her ankle, pulled on jeans and T-shirt, released her hair from its pins and tied it back with a length of blue ribbon. The doorbell rang while she was seeking inspiration about supper, and with a sigh she shut the fridge and lifted the receiver, hoping it wasn't Claire or Ellie, or anyone else intent on cheering her up.

'Yes?'

'Let me in, Laura, *per favore.*'

She stared at the receiver in shock. 'You're not in Venice?' she said idiotically, and Domenico laughed.

'No, Laura. I am right here, outside your building.'

She pressed the release button in a daze, and opened her door to watch him taking the stairs, two at a time. He was wearing his wonderful leather jacket with jeans that had probably come from the same source as his suits. His glossy dark hair was a little ruffled for once, but his chin was newly shaved and Laura could have eaten him on toast. He smiled at her, looking so outrageously pleased with himself she laughed up at him with equal pleasure.

'You said you would dine with me when I am in London,' he said, and kissed her uninjured cheek. 'So. Here I am.'

She closed the door behind them, eyeing him quizzically. 'You didn't say tonight! I was hoping to look rather more human before we met again.'

He scowled. 'Do you really believe such things matter to me? I could not leave for Venice knowing you still believe this lie about another woman in my life!'

Laura looked up into the jewel-bright blue eyes and saw truth in them, along with something else that made her heart beat faster. 'If you say it's a lie I believe you.'

He moved closer. 'There is no one. *E verita*, Laura. I had so much looked forward to seeing you at the wedding, and felt great shock to find you missing. And when I did see you—'

'You were revolted. I saw the look in your eyes.'

'This is not true! I felt only anguish that you had suffered such pain. And this also,' he added fiercely, 'is not a lie.'

'Then I apologise.'

'*Grazie.*' He smiled ruefully. 'But I was not truthful about the subject of our relationship.'

'You said it was boring,' she reminded him.

He threw out his hands. 'This was retaliation. I came to you to arrange our lives to spend as much time together as possible, and you accuse me of having another woman!'

'I'm sorry,' she said penitently.

'*Bene.*' His eyes narrowed to an unsettling gleam. 'I insist that you make this up to me.'

She smiled demurely. 'How can I do that?'

'You are flirting with me, Laura,' he said, delighted. 'You know exactly how. If you have forgotten, I will take great pleasure in showing you. But not,' he added with deep regret, 'until next time we meet. Tonight I am afraid to hurt you if I even kiss you.'

'I don't think one kiss would hurt too much,' she whispered, and Domenico took her in his arms and laid his lips on hers with gentleness that transformed into warmth as she responded with fervour fuelled by relief that he was here and she was in his arms where she belonged. When he released her mouth at last he drew her close, careful of her injured face.

'Tell me you are sorry for being so cruel to me,' he commanded unevenly.

'You got off lightly. When Fen told me you had a woman in your life I was ready to kill you,' she said fiercely, and Domenico gave a deep-throated growl of male satisfaction.

'You were jealous!' He kissed her nose. 'I like this *very* much.'

She smiled ruefully. 'It was a first for me, and I hated it.'

He took a look around the small room, and tossed his jacket on a chair. 'Come. Let us sit down together and I shall tell you why your jealousy, much as it delights me, was unnecessary.' He drew her down on the sofa, smiling as she apologised for its size. 'I am glad of it because we must sit very close together.'

Laura was glad, too. It was bliss to sit with Domenico's arm round her, breathing in the scent of him. The scent she would know in the dark. 'So why did Jess Forli think there was someone in your life?'

'She rang me to tell me where to stay for Fenella's wedding.' Domenico's arm tightened. 'And Jess asked me, as she always does, if I had someone special in my life yet. And this time I said yes, but would not give her a name.' He turned her face up to his. 'I thought it best to consult you first, *tesoro*.'

Laura stared at him. 'You mean it was me?'

He kissed her parted mouth fleetingly. 'Of course it was you!'

'I was jealous of myself?'

'Who else would it be? I am in love with *you*, Laura, only you. And because you wanted to kill me,' he added with satisfaction, 'you are in love with me, yes?'

'Hopelessly!'

Domenico shook his head. 'Our situation is not hopeless at all, *innamorata*.'

'It was after you stormed out of my house the day of the wedding!'

His eyes kindled. 'I came to comfort you, and you accused me of lies and threw money at me. What man would not be angry?'

'Sorry, Domenico,' she said, so meekly he laughed and tugged on her hair.

'So meek and mild, but I know better.' He raised her hand to his lips, then stood up and pulled her with him. 'Now, tell me where we can dine. I am hungry.'

Laura shook her head firmly. 'I'm not going out like this.' She grinned. 'I do a great omelette—remember?'

'I will never forget. And I will enjoy another very much.' He took her in his arms and rubbed his cheek against her hair. 'I am hungry for so much more than food, Laura, but I am afraid to hurt you.'

She tipped her head back to look at him. 'It didn't hurt when you kissed me. And my ankle doesn't hurt when I'm lying down.'

Domenico's breathing quickened. 'You mean this?'

'With all my heart,' she assured him breathlessly, and smiled into his blazing eyes as he picked her up and carried her into the bedroom.

He undressed her as though he were unwrapping a priceless gift, and made love to her with exquisite gentleness that was just as rapturous in its own way as the heat and passion of the first time. And later, after sharing a vast omelette with her, Domenico made it clear to Laura that in future their lives must be arranged to allow as much time together as humanly possible.

'If you love me, *carissima*,' he said as he finally left her, 'come to me in Venice very soon.'

'I do, and I will,' she promised, and stood on tiptoe for one last kiss.

*   *   *

The surprise visit from Domenico did more for Laura's face and frame of mind than any medication. Within days her face was less painful, soon she was able to disguise her fading bruises with cosmetics, and there were no more problems with concentration during her working day. She received postcards from Abby in France, from her mother in the Lakes, and the newlyweds in Italy, but her regular phone calls from Domenico were the highlights of her days. She was so much happier with life it caused comment on the trading floor at the bank, with demands about who was the lucky guy.

'I wondered why he wanted your London address,' said her mother, when she heard the phone was a present from Domenico. 'If you've kept it I take it things are more cordial between you now?'

'Much more. He came to see me and explained a few things.'

'Did he, indeed? I take it there is no lady in his life?'

'Other than me, no. So I'm off to Venice again once I can get more time off. I shan't need a hotel; I'll stay with Domenico in his apartment.'

'Well, well, things *are* more cordial.'

'He rings me up a lot to make sure they stay that way. How's Janet?'

'She's wearing me out. I haven't done so much walking in years.'

Laura laughed. 'You'll be fit as a fiddle by the time you come home. And Abby's obviously having a ball in France by her postcards. I'm glad. She deserves it.'

Domenico was unable to leave Venice again at the height of the tourist season, and Laura, wanting more than a snatched weekend break, had to wait until the middle of September before she could take more time off from the bank. In the

meantime she'd been home to Stavely for a celebration dinner to mark the newlyweds' return and admire the wedding
presents, and Isabel and Abby had come to London for a day
so that the three of them could hit the shops together to stock
Abby up for college.

'At last!' exclaimed Domenico, when Laura told him her
flight was booked. 'I am tired of waiting. It is a very long
time since we were together.'

Laura could have told him to the minute just how long.
'Can you keep the entire week free?'

'Every second of it, *carissima*. Is your face truly healed
now?'

'Like new,' she assured him.

'Ah, Laura, now that my time of waiting is nearly over I
cannot wait to hold you in my arms again.'

'Just two more weeks,' she said huskily.

'I will be waiting at Marco Polo.'

'In a less impatient mood than last time, I hope!'

He laughed softly. 'I shall be even more impatient to rush
you to a boat again, but this time to a water taxi, for the
fastest journey possible to my apartment.'

By which, thought Laura happily, Domenico meant to
make love to her the moment they were through his door.
With this in mind she went on a shopping expedition with
money her mother had given her from her windfall, and spent
a shamelessly large part of it on underwear.

Laura went down to Stavely regularly, but during one
weekend she'd stayed in the flat the doorbell rang while she
was enjoying the luxury of a late breakfast with the Sunday
papers.

'It's me,' said a hoarse little voice through the intercom.
'Let me in, please.'

'*Abby?*' Laura pressed the release button and opened the
door to see her sister creeping up the stairs in such obvious

pain she flew down to help her. 'What on earth's the matter, love? Have you hurt yourself? Where's Mother?'

When her only answer was a visceral groan, Laura put an arm round Abby's waist and helped her up to the flat. 'Tell me what's wrong,' she said urgently.

'*Bathroom,*' gasped Abby, and staggered through the door Laura opened for her.

When she heard anguished groans Laura disregarded her frantic pleas for privacy and went in after Abby, her practical side taking over when it dawned on her what was happening. She soaked a hand towel in cold water to bathe Abby's sweating face, and unable to help in any other way, held her sister's hand until the inexorable process was over. She turned on the shower and helped the shocked, sobbing girl out of her clothes, and when Abby was clean and dry wrapped her in a dressing gown and made her lie on the bed to recover.

Laura went to the kitchen to make tea, but Abby slid off the bed to follow her, looking at her with huge reddened eyes, her face ashen beneath its suntan.

'I'm sorry about landing you with this,' she said unsteadily.

'Don't worry about that,' said Laura firmly. 'The important thing right now is to get you to a hospital—'

'*No,*' wailed Abby, sounding more like eight than eighteen.

'I'm afraid you must, love. Don't worry, the hospital's quite near. I'll give you something to wear, then I'll ring Mother and bring her up to speed.'

'Don't do that!' said Abby frantically. 'I don't want her to know.'

'Of course she must know,' said Laura gently. 'Where does she think you are now?'

'Out for the day with Rachel.'

'And where does Rachel think you are?'

'Up here for the day with you.'

'You were taking a chance!'

'I was desperate,' sobbed Abby.

Laura put a comforting arm round her. 'Don't cry. I know you feel rough, but get these clothes on, love. The taxi should be here any minute.'

With a feeling of *déjà vu* Laura reported at Reception in the A & E department, but Abby keeled over while they were taking her details, which meant that she was wheeled away immediately. While her sister was examined Laura rang her mother, who took the news on the chin and said she would start out at once for the flat, in case Abby was allowed out of hospital before she got there.

On her way back to her sister Laura's heart sank when a familiar white-coated figure came striding towards her.

'Laura! Is something wrong?' demanded Edward Lassiter.

Not with me, she thought glumly. 'I'm fine. I'm just here with someone.'

His hazel eyes studied her face closely. 'Your face has healed well. It was a hell of a shock to see you covered in contusions.'

'It was to me, too,' she said dryly.

'Could we meet for a drink some time?' he asked in an undertone, but before Laura could answer his name was called urgently. 'I'll be in touch,' he promised as he hurried away.

When Laura got back to Abby it wrung her heart to see her lively, clever young sister lying like a marble effigy in the bed. 'Hi,' she said, more cheerfully than she felt. 'How do you feel?'

'Not so hot.' Abby tried to smile. 'But at least I don't need a surgical procedure. They're giving me some drug. I'll be discharged this evening at the latest.'

'That's good.'

'Have you rung Ma?'

'Yes. She's on her way.'

'Oh, God!' The amber eyes shut tight in anguish for a moment then opened to look straight into Laura's. 'I didn't do anything to make this happen, but I wanted to. I came to ask you how to get a termination.'

Laura went cold. 'Not something I'm clued up about, I'm afraid.'

Abby swallowed hard. 'A good thing nature did it for me, then. I was up at the crack of dawn to walk to Chepstow to catch the London coach, but I was in the underground from Victoria when I started getting these awful cramps. I thought maybe the pregnancy test was wrong and it was just the usual thing. But on the way to the flat I realised it was more than that and I really panicked, thinking I'd never make it before...' She dissolved into bitter, painful sobs, and Laura bent to kiss her as she mopped her up.

'Don't, love. You got to me in time, thank God.'

'And you just took over without a fuss.' Abby sniffed hard. 'You were great, sis. Thank you.'

Laura braced herself. 'Can I ask who's responsible?'

'I am.' The drawn young face turned mulish. 'I made a big mistake.'

'It takes two, love.'

'I don't want to talk about it.' Tears started again, and Laura patted her sister's hand reassuringly.

'I'll go back to wait for Mother, and then we'll both come to collect you later. Are you all right with that?'

Abby nodded miserably. 'Sorry I made such a mess of things.'

'Don't think like that.' Laura gave her sister a fierce look. 'Now, listen to me, Abigail Green. You put this behind you, go off to Trinity next month, and just get on with your life.'

Domenico rang as Laura was letting herself into the flat. 'How are you, *tesoro*?'

'I'm fine,' she assured him, wishing she could let him into Abby's sad little secret. 'How are you?'

'I am well, but you sound tired, *amore*.'

'I've had things to do. Mother and Abby will be with me soon for a visit,' said Laura, needing to tell him at least part of the truth.

'You will enjoy that. Please give your mother my regards. Even on such brief acquaintance I find her most *simpatica*.'

'You've hardly known me any longer.'

'Long enough to know that you and I are meant for each other. *Per sempre*,' he added, in a tone that buckled her knees.

'Forever?'

'Yes, Laura, forever. When you come to me I shall take great pleasure in convincing you of this!'

Later that night, after Abby had been settled in bed at the flat, Laura ordered her exhausted, wrung-out mother to sit still while she made supper. 'Just sit there on the sofa and I'll wait on you.'

'That's very sweet of you, darling, but I don't feel very hungry.'

'I know, but you must eat something,' said Laura firmly. 'Abby's agreed to some soup, and I'll whip up a couple of my special omelettes.'

Isabel straightened her shoulders. 'You're right. I'll need all the energy I can get when I go home. Abby will heal quickly enough physically, but I'll have to watch that she gets over it mentally, too.'

'University will help with that.'

'Practical Laura, as always! And thank God you are, darling. This can't have been a pleasant experience for you.'

'It was a lot worse for Abby.' Laura shook her head in wonder. 'She hiked to Chepstow to catch the London coach this morning.'

'Over three miles in that condition! And I thought she was off to the Kents for a day out with Rachel.' Isabel looked at Laura in despair. 'Why didn't she tell me what was wrong?'

'Look at it from her point of view,' said Laura gently. 'Up to now Abby's been the perfect daughter, never a moment's trouble of any kind. Then this happened. She obviously felt she'd ruined your life as well as hers.'

'I can see your point,' sighed Isabel. 'But what on earth made her trek all the way to London to see you?'

'She wanted my support,' said Laura, sparing her mother the real reason. She frowned. 'I haven't heard about any boyfriend. I asked who was responsible but she wouldn't say. Any ideas?'

'Not a clue.' Isabel thrust an agitated hand through her hair. 'She spends the night at the Kents' house sometimes, and Rachel comes to us, and they both go to parties and out with friends. But Abby tends to frighten boys off because she's so clever. I shouldn't have let her work at the café,' she added despairingly. 'She must have met someone there.'

'Perhaps she'll tell you tomorrow.'

'If she wouldn't tell you, I doubt it.' Isabel looked at her daughter with sudden compunction. 'This was a lot for you to cope with on your own. I'm so sorry, darling.'

'Don't be.' Laura smiled reassuringly. 'You and Abby can stay here until she feels better. Then you just say you've both spent a few days in London with me, and no one need know a thing about it back in Stavely.'

'Do you think I care a damn about that?' said Isabel fiercely.

'No. But Abby obviously does, quite desperately, so we'll just have to respect that.' Laura's eyes glittered malevolently. 'This morning, when it was all happening, I could have killed the man who put her through this, whoever he is.'

'Laura, please ask her again. Abby will find it easier to

tell you than me,' said Isabel urgently. 'All the way up in the car I kept thinking about rape. I need to know.'

Laura heated some soup and made fingers of toast, and took a tray into her bedroom, prepared to feed Abby if necessary. But, with the resilience of youth, particularly one who hadn't eaten since the evening before, the invalid confessed to feeling hungry.

'I must have a really shallow nature to want food after—after all that,' she said as Laura stacked pillows behind her.

'Sensible, not shallow. You need nourishment. And I open a pretty damn fine tin of soup, if I do say so myself.'

Having won a weak smile from the invalid, Laura went back to the kitchen to make the promised omelettes, pleased when her mother obediently ate hers.

During the meal Isabel suggested Laura shared her bed with Abby. 'I'll take the sofa. I'm hoping she might confide in you.'

'Or she might get so upset neither of us will sleep a wink.'

'I know. It's a lot to ask of you, darling, but I can't rest until I know what happened. I'll take some tea to her in a minute.'

Isabel looked stricken when she returned.

'What's wrong?' asked Laura.

'Abby was so openly relieved about the sleeping arrangements.'

It was late by the time both Laura's house guests had been settled for the night, and she was tired when she slid carefully into bed beside her sister.

'I'm told I don't snore, so you should be able to sleep.'

Abby sighed. 'I don't expect to sleep much, Laurie—how do you know you don't snore?'

'Domenico told me.'

'You've slept with him, then?'

'Yes.'

Silence for a while.

'Did you actually like it?' blurted Abby. 'The sex, I mean?'

Careful, thought Laura. 'I'm very much in love with him. There were feelings and emotions involved. It wasn't just sex.'

'Well, if that's all it takes to get pregnant I'm never going to have sex again, ever,' said Abby bitterly.

'It was just the once, then?'

'Once was enough!'

'Look, Abby, please tell me who it was. Mother's desperately worried.'

'I can't!'

'She thinks you were raped.'

Abby swallowed audibly. 'It depends on what you mean by rape. I wasn't attacked with a knife held to my throat, or anything. I thought he wanted a goodnight kiss or two, and I was up for that. Am I stupid, or what? A few French kisses, a lot of groping and bingo! He was in a real state afterwards, because it was my first time and he hurt me.' She gave a sarcastic little laugh. 'My virginity was such a surprise it knocked him for six. Anyway, he said I needn't worry about catching anything, and made a joke about jail-bait—' She stopped dead.

'And he'd know all about that, of course, because he's a lawyer!' Laura's hands clenched. 'He also happens to be your best friend's brother, and you're very fond of Mrs Kent.'

'You can see why I didn't want anyone to know,' said Abby despairingly. 'Will you tell Ma it was Marcus?'

'No, you will. She needs to know. But don't worry. If you want it kept secret it will be. I suppose it happened the night he took you to the concert?'

'Yes, but it rained so much we went back to his car before the end. I was wearing the T-shirt you gave me, with my new miniskirt, and I was flattered because he was so complimentary. On the way home he stopped the car in a lane and—'

'I can fill in the rest. Bastard!' said Laura fiercely.

'No, he's not. He's actually very nice. But he's so much older than me I just never dreamed he'd fancy me like that.'

Laura pictured her long-legged sister in the scarlet T-shirt and brief skirt and knew exactly why Marcus Kent had fancied her. 'Mother will be relieved in one way, at least, and no one else will ever know. You can go off to college and forget it ever happened.'

Abby gave a cynical laugh. 'At least Mother won't have to worry about me in that way when I'm up at Trinity. I'll never let a man near me again.'

Laura reached for her hand. 'Accidents can still happen, Abby. Take a leaf out of my book and get sorted out with contraceptive pills a.s.a.p.'

CHAPTER NINE

WHEN Laura arrived home from work the following evening she found Abby and her mother packed and ready to leave.

'So soon?' she said, surprised.

'Ma needs to get back to school,' said Abby. 'She refuses to let me sleep on the sofa, and I'm sure I'm keeping you awake, sis, so I've persuaded my chauffeur to drive me home.'

'It's best all round,' said Isabel. 'Abby will be happier in her own bed, with her own things around her.'

'I can pretend everything's back to normal,' said Abby sardonically.

Laura looked her in the eye. 'Everything, as you put it, could be a whole lot worse.'

Abby flushed. 'I know. You've been a real star, Laura, and I am grateful, honestly. It's just—'

'I know. You've had a very sobering experience and you're feeling low. Your hormones have taken a bashing, remember. And you look very peaky—all eyes. How do you feel? Really?'

'A bit wishy-washy, but I'll live.'

'Abby's worried about seeing Rachel and her family,' explained Isabel. 'But she must carry on as usual. The Kents were kind enough to take her to France with them, after all.'

'Just make sure you're otherwise engaged when Marcus is home,' said Laura, eyes kindling.

'Don't worry, he won't want a replay,' said Abby. 'It was a one-off, in every sense of the word. Just thinking about it gives me the shivers. But as long as no one knows about it I can cope. So don't you dare tell Fenny.'

'Not a word.' Laura turned to her mother. 'And how are *you* feeling?'

Isabel smiled ruefully. 'A bit arthritic! That sofa of yours makes a very uncomfortable bed.'

'You should have swapped with me,' said Abby impatiently.

'You're a lot taller than I am. Right, then, sweetheart, the traffic should have calmed down a bit so let's make a start. You can go straight to bed when we get home.'

Abby hugged Laura, suddenly tearful. 'Come down again soon.'

'I will. Now, eat properly, take it easy, and get yourself fit for next month.' Laura turned to her mother. 'And you take care of yourself, too. You're the only mother we've got.'

'Tough as old boots, me,' said Isabel cheerfully. 'I did some shopping this afternoon, to make sure you had a meal tonight, Laura. Goodbye, darling. I'll ring as soon as we get home.'

Laura went down to the basement car park to see them off, then went back up to the flat, which felt very quiet and empty now she was alone. Her only consolation was the thought that in less than ten days she would be in Venice with Domenico.

Fate decreed otherwise. The following week an epidemic of summer flu hit the bank and Laura, one of the few not to succumb, was asked to postpone her holiday until staff shortages were less acute. Bitterly disappointed, she rang Domenico that evening and told him her trip was off for the time being.

'*Cosa?*' he said explosively. 'Laura, how can you do this to me? I have been counting the days.'

'So have I,' she assured him huskily. 'I'll come as soon as I can, I promise. I'm disappointed, too. I'm so sorry, Domenico…' She sniffed hard.

'Ah, *carissima*, forgive me. I know it is not your fault. Do not cry. It gives me much pain when it is not possible to hold you in my arms and kiss away your tears…' Domenico went on talking, his voice huskier and his accent pronounced as he told her a great many gratifying things that made her feel a lot better by the time they said goodnight.

Laura felt even better the following evening. She arrived at the flat late after an extra-hard day in work, feeling depressed because she should have been flying to Venice next day. While she was considering her options of a swim in the pool or a hot bath with a book as the evening's entertainment Domenico rang, two hours earlier than usual.

'*Come esta*, Laura?'

'Tired. I've just come in. It was a long, long day. How are you?'

'I am very pleased with myself.'

Laura chuckled. 'Why? What's happened?'

'I cannot wait for more weeks before I see you. I am flying to Heathrow on Friday and I shall stay at my usual hotel. I have some business to attend to during the afternoon, but for the rest of the weekend I shall be free. I have booked a double room. Share it with me, *tesoro*. We shall have time together, but in London instead of Venice.'

Laura's eyes widened in delight. 'Domenico, what a wonderful idea! I'd love it. I live in London but I've never stayed in a hotel here.'

'Then come to me straight from your bank on Friday.'

Laura paid off the taxi in the forecourt of the famous hotel, glowing with anticipation as she took out her phone. 'I'm here,' she said when Domenico answered.

'*Amore!* At last. Hurry!'

He gave her his room number, and Laura crossed the palatial lobby to the lifts, her excitement mounting as she watched the floor numbers flash by. When the lift arrived at his floor Domenico was standing in the open doorway to his room, arms flung wide in welcome. Laura ran into them and they closed about her tightly for a moment before he turned her face up to his.

'I look a bit better now,' she said breathlessly.

Domenico put her bag on the floor and closed the door, his eyes moving over her face like a caress. 'You are perfect.'

She smiled ruefully. 'If you want perfect I'm the wrong woman.'

He shook his head. 'You are the right woman—the only woman—for me, Laura.'

'Then why aren't you kissing me?'

He seized her in his arms, rubbing his cheek against her hair. 'I am afraid to hurt you, *tesoro*.'

Laura reached up to lock her hands behind his neck. 'The only way to hurt me is to refuse to kiss me!'

Their lips met with a relishing sigh of pleasure, but instead of devouring her as Laura had half expected Domenico pressed a series of gentle kisses over the healed part of her face before returning to her mouth. When her lips parted in eager response his tongue became urgent, and her heart began to pound as he held her close against his own heartbeat, which accelerated as their kisses grew wilder and breathing grew laboured, until suddenly Domenico let her go, breathing raggedly.

'I waited here instead of coming down to meet you, so that I would not shock other guests by making love to you in the foyer,' he said unevenly. '*Scusa, tesoro*, I have not even said words of welcome.'

'You made me feel very welcome without them,' she assured him breathlessly, and smiled. 'But also very warm.'

'Then I will take this off.' He undid the buttons on her black jacket and slid it from her shoulders. 'You are very elegant, Laura.'

She smiled demurely. 'I thought the occasion—and this

hotel—demanded it, so I changed into a dress at work before I left. Is it suitable to go down to dinner?'

'It is delightful,' he said, surveying the clinging caramel jersey. 'But we are not going down to dinner. We shall make use of Room Service if this is agreeable to you,' he added, his eyes glinting.

She smiled radiantly. 'Very agreeable!'

Domenico laid her jacket on the bed and took her hand to lead her to a large chair near the window. He sat down and drew her onto his lap, cradling her against his shoulder. 'So tell me about your family. Are they well?'

Yes, thank God, thought Laura. 'Mother's back in school and Abby's getting ready for Cambridge.'

'She will enjoy the student life, you think? It must be hard for your mother to part with her.'

'She'll find the house very quiet for a while, but I go down there at weekends whenever I can.'

'Does your mother know you are here with me this weekend?'

'Of course.' Laura smiled up at him. 'My feelings for you are no secret.'

'I am very happy to hear this.' He turned her face up to his to kiss her. 'We must have no more secrets between us, yes?'

'You were the one with the secret, not me!'

'You will never let me forget this,' he said, resigned, and stroked a finger down her cheek. 'Is there some way I can make it up to you?'

'I'll try to think of one.'

'I could do this,' he said, and kissed her fingers one by one. 'Or this.' He trailed his mouth down her cheek and throat, causing shivers down her spine. 'You are cold?'

'No, I'm hot,' she said breathlessly. 'What else can you do?'

Domenico set her on her feet and stood up. 'I can give

you two choices. I ring for dinner now, or I take you to bed and we eat later.'

Laura gave him a smile that made him blink. 'That's no choice. I vote for bed.'

He crushed her to him. '*Ti amo*, Laura.'

She gazed up at him, remembering Fen's confidences. 'I love you too, so much it hurts.'

Domenico's eyes blazed. 'Then show me, *amore*.'

Keeping her eyes on his, Laura backed away and reached behind her to undo her zip. Domenico made a move to help her, but she shook her head, smiling, watching his eyes dilate as she stepped out of the dress wearing outrageously provocative scraps of lace-edged nude chiffon so sheer her nipples were clearly visible as they hardened in response to the heat in his eyes. With a growl he scooped her up to lay her on the bed, his lips and tongue caressing her through the fabric as his fingers slid up her thigh to find the heat pulsing behind the triangle of chiffon that grew damp as he found the small, erect bud beneath it.

'Domenico!' she gasped, writhing under the caress, and he tore himself away to strip off his clothes. He kissed her knees, then gently parted them to lie between her thighs as he pressed kisses all over her face and down her throat, pausing for a moment in the hollow between her breasts before he renewed his attentions to the thinly veiled nipples that were so sensitive to the touch Laura could hardly bear it. She reached out a questing hand to retaliate, but he closed his fingers round her wrist.

'Touch me and I am lost,' he panted, and laid a trail of open-mouthed kisses down her quivering body. He peeled the damp scrap of chiffon away at last, to replace it with his lips and seeking tongue, and Laura gasped and clutched at his hair, and Domenico slid back up her body and entered it with a sure, triumphant thrust she felt in every part of her as his eyes blazed down into hers. She smiled into them, tightening inner muscles around him in response, and he kissed her deeply, gripping her hip bones as they moved together, their mutual arousal so intense the orgasm they experienced almost in unison left them shaken and speechless, clutching each other for support as the throbbing died away.

At last Domenico raised his head to smile down into Laura's face, smoothing damp tendrils of hair from her face. 'What are you thinking, *tesoro*?'

Laura shook her head, her eyes still dazed. 'I never dreamed that sex could be like that, Domenico.'

'But it is not just sex for us,' he said huskily. 'It is my heart making love to your heart. Or is that too romantic for my practical Laura?'

She shook her head. 'From anyone else it would be, but from you, no, Domenico.'

'That is good. But do not talk of anyone else! You are mine.' He kissed her possessively by way of emphasis. 'And to show I can also be practical, what would you like to eat?'

'That means you're hungry, not practical!'

'A man must eat,' he said, and slid his hands behind her to unhook the bra she'd forgotten she was wearing. He tossed it aside and bent to kiss each hard little peak, but then drew back regretfully, shaking his head. 'We must eat before we love again.'

'And you can't get more practical than that,' she teased, revelling in Domenico's reaction when she sat up and deliberately arched her back as she took the escaping pins from her hair.

'The eating can be postponed,' he warned, his eyes darkening, but when he reached for her she laughed and scooted across the broad bed to stand at the far side, shaking her hair down like a scarf to act as cover. 'My Botticelli *Venus*!' exclaimed Domenico, but Laura shook her head.

'I'm real, not a painting, and I want a shower before we eat. Do you have a dressing gown I can borrow?'

Later, wrapped in white towelling robes provided by the hotel, they shared lobster and strawberries, drank a little of the celebration champagne Domenico had ordered and talked non-stop, telling each other everything that had happened in the time spent apart.

'It is a pity you could not come to Venice,' said Domenico, feeding Laura a strawberry. 'My parents want so much to meet you.'

Her eyes widened. 'Really?'

'I have met with your mother,' he pointed out.

'I know, but—'

'Does she like me?'

'Well, yes, she does, but—'

'And my parents will like you,' he informed her. 'They invite you to their house in Umbria next time you come.'

'But, Domenico—'

'You are very fond of this word "but",' he said, and leaned over to kiss her. 'I have told my parents about you, so naturally they wish to meet you.'

Laura eyed him apprehensively. 'What, exactly, have you told them?'

'That I have met this beautiful young lady who looks like a princess from a fairy tale with her long golden hair, and who works in banking in London's Docklands. They were most impressed, also very happy for me.' He smiled wryly. 'Since Alessa I have shown no interest in commitment, you understand.'

'Commitment?'

'Is it so frightening a word?' He stroked a fingertip down her cheek. 'I am very much in love with you, Laura. These stolen moments together are sweet but not enough for me. I want you in my life all the time.'

Laura's mind went round in circles as she watched Domenico load the trolley and push it outside the door. What did he mean by 'all the time'?

'You do that very expertly,' she commented as he rejoined her on the bed.

'It is no surprise that I do. My father was a hard taskmaster. In vacations from college I worked in the hotel kitchens, carried luggage to rooms, waited on tables once I was considered fit to do so, acted as barman, receptionist.' He threw out his hands. 'I did not change beds or clean rooms, but otherwise I have done most things.'

She picked up one of the slim, beautiful hands. 'Yet this looks as though it's never done more than sign your name.'

He shrugged. 'You may call it vanity, but it is a matter of pride for me to look as good as I can.'

'Then you can understand my feelings when you surprised me in scruffy old clothes in the garden, with my hair hanging down!'

'It is hanging down right now.'

'That's different.'

He frowned. 'You are changing the subject, Laura. You do not want to be with me all the time?'

She sighed. 'Yes, I do. But the cautious, practical side of me says we haven't known each other long enough to make plans of that kind.'

Domenico raised her up against the stacked pillows and sat cross-legged, facing her. 'So. How long must we know each other before you will come to me? Weeks, months? You are little more than a child, of course—'

'I'm twenty-three!'

'But I am thirty-four. Until I met you I did not miss a woman's presence in my life. But now my apartment feels empty without you. So does my life.' He moved nearer, his eyes intent on hers. 'It is a waste of valuable time to spend so much of it apart, *amore*.'

'I know, but it would be a very big step for me to take.'

'You would be sad to leave your mother and sister,' he

said, nodding. 'But Venice is not far. They could fly to see you as often as they wish.'

'What sort of timescale do you have in mind?'

'In January I usually take a skiing holiday.' He smiled persuasively. 'It can be our honeymoon.'

Laura's eyes widened. 'You mean you want to marry me?'

In one lithe movement Domenico was beside her. He took her in his arms, smiling into her startled eyes. 'Is this so great a surprise? Should I have served a diamond ring with the lobster to convince you?'

She shook her head, smiling. 'I'm surprised because you told me that Alessa had put you right off marriage.'

'This was true. Then you came to Venice and changed my mind—and my heart!'

She kissed him fervently by way of thanks then frowned suddenly. 'Are you a Catholic, Domenico?'

'Yes, though not as devout as my mother would wish.'

'Then this could be a problem.'

He shrugged. 'I would not ask you to change your own faith, Laura, though our children would naturally be raised in mine.'

'Whoa!' she said breathlessly. 'Not so fast. Let's sort ourselves out before we go on to the subject of children.'

Domenico leaned back against the stacked pillows, holding Laura close. 'Now we are comfortable to do this sorting out.'

'First of all,' she began, determined to be practical, 'we haven't known each other long.'

'This may be a problem for you, *amore*, but it is not for me.' He turned her face up to his to kiss her. 'So what is the second problem?'

'Your religion looks on marriage as permanent—no divorce allowed.'

'Divorce will not be a problem for us,' Domenico assured her. 'Once you are my wife I will never let you go.'

Ninety per cent of Laura was thrilled to bits with this declaration. But ten per cent warned that it was only sensible to get to know each other better before burning her boats so finally. 'I want very much to marry you one day, Domenico—'

'But,' he said, resigned. 'You like this word too much,' he said again.

She looked at him squarely. 'If we rush things you might regret it, and feel trapped in a marriage you no longer want. And because we are both human and fallible and come from different cultures this might well happen—'

'And we could both grow wings and fly to the moon, but none of this *will* happen,' interrupted Domenico, and kissed her fiercely. 'Do you love me?'

'Yes, but—'

'No more buts.' He kissed her again. 'Because I adore you, Laura *mia*, I will give you a little time to get used to the idea, but not too much. I am not a patient man.'

'I noticed that the first time we met,' she said dryly.

He smiled and threaded his hands through her hair. 'I saw a young girl in a white sunhat and dark glasses which hid her face, and instead of recognising my fate felt only relief because the tourist I had been ordered to meet arrived on time.'

'Ordered?'

'Lorenzo can be very imperious! I was not pleased to take time from a very unpleasant situation to meet Fenella's friend. But later that night, when I met you at Florian's, I was very pleased indeed, and most grateful to my cousin,' he assured her, and caressed her earlobe with the tip of his tongue.

She gave a little shiver and wriggled closer. 'I certainly didn't think you were *my* fate at Marco Polo, even if you were the best-looking man I'd ever met.'

'You thought that?' he said, delighted.

'Oh, yes. And that was before I saw the eyes behind the

sunglasses. Those baby blues of yours pack quite a punch,
Domenico Chiesa!'

'If they attracted you to me I thank God for it,' he said
fervently.

'What was the situation that made you so impatient to get
rid of me?' she asked curiously.

'A guest at the hotel had accused one of the cleaners of
stealing a valuable ring, and I had to leave the problem unresolved to go to Marco Polo.'

'Ah, I see. What happened when you got back?'

'During my absence the guest had found her ring. Her
husband was very embarrassed. He offered money to Anna,
but with much dignity she refused.'

'Good for her! Does she still work for you?'

'Of course. She is very loyal.'

'And she trusted you to be loyal to her?'

Domenico nodded gravely. 'Trust yourself to me in the
same way, *amante*, and I swear I will never give you cause
to regret it.'

Laura put her arms round his neck. 'If I do marry you—'

'When you marry me,' he corrected.

'What will I do with myself? I'm used to working. You
know I love your apartment, but I can't just sit there all day
twiddling my thumbs until you come home.'

'If you wish you could work in the hotel with me.' He
smiled in sudden inspiration. 'You can lighten my workload
and be my very own personal assistant.'

'Sounds tempting, but there's a language problem, remember? I learnt a little Italian in school but I'm far from fluent,'
she warned, secretly rather thrilled with the idea.

'You can take more lessons during this time that you are
making me wait.' Domenico drew her into his arms. 'But I
can teach you the most important words right now. Say after
me. *Ti amo*, Domenico.'

'*Ti amo*, Domenico,' she repeated fervently. '*Ti amo per
sempre.*'

CHAPTER TEN

AFTER a lavish breakfast with Domenico next morning Laura made a proposition that surprised him.

'It must cost an arm and a leg here,' she said, refilling their coffee-cups. 'How would you like to spend the rest of your stay in my flat? Think of the money it would save.'

Domenico's eyebrows rose. 'You would prefer this?'

'Yes. How about you?'

He shrugged, smiling. 'To be with you is all I desire, Laura—it matters little where we are. You wish to go now?'

'Yes, because we need to go shopping for food. You don't have to come with me for that,' she added.

'You know that I enjoy shopping with you, *tesoro*.'

'But that was in Venice. You'll find it a bit different in Bow!'

'I will enjoy it just the same. But first give me the pleasure of watching you dress.' Domenico smiled at her look of surprise. 'I would consider this a great privilege.'

Laura found it oddly erotic to put on underwear, even the less provocative kind she normally wore, with Domenico's eyes following the process. Her colour high, she put on a fresh white shirt and the tailored black trouser suit she'd worn to work the previous day. Her fingers were all thumbs as she coiled her hair up, but at last she did her face and slid her feet into her shoes. 'There,' she said. 'Done.'

'You wear these clothes to the bank?' said Domenico, getting up.

'Yes.'

'Then now I understand why you are Ice Maiden.' He raised her hand to his lips. 'I think this severe look is very sexy, *tesoro*, and want to kiss much more than your hand. But if I do, this robe will shed its whiteness all over your suit.'

'You could take it off,' she said, then fended him off, laughing, as he promptly tossed the robe on the floor and snatched her in his arms. 'No, Domenico, *please*, or I'll have to start all over again.'

When the taxi deposited them outside Laura's building later Domenico took their luggage into the lift and once the doors closed on them kissed her as though they'd been parted for months.

'It is a whole hour since I did that,' he said when they reached her floor.

'We need to go shopping for food,' Laura reminded him breathlessly, and Domenico frowned.

'Then I should have kept the taxi. I have no car this time.'

'We walk,' she informed him, and grinned at his look of dismay. 'A couple of carrier bags should be a doddle with those skier's muscles of yours.'

'A doddle? What is that?'

'It means it should be very easy for you.'

'I shall do whatever you want,' he assured her. 'But first I wish to unpack my clothes.'

'Nice to know where your priorities lie!' she teased, laughing.

It was a surprisingly intimate process to make room among her own clothes for Domenico's. When the contents of his suit bag hung in the wardrobe and the rest of his clothes were folded away in drawers with hers, Laura turned to meet a look in his eyes that told her the feeling was mutual. He held out his arms and she leaned into them, but after a few moments Domenico sighed deeply, kissed her forehead and gently pushed her away.

'Now we buy this food, yes?'

'Yes.'

It was a bright, sunny day, with a sharp, autumnal edge to it, and Laura felt so happy she wanted to sing as Domenico held her hand on the walk to the supermarket. But once they started filling a shopping trolley she had to remind him constantly that her storage space was limited and her refrigerator small. Brushing aside her protests, he insisted on buying an expensive Italian coffee machine to make the Italian coffee he found.

'The machine can live on your kitchen counter, Laura. I do not like instant coffee.'

Rather than get into a pitched battle in public she gave in, mainly because she loved good coffee as much as he did. But she dug her heels in about the other things on her list.

'I need basics like butter, bread and milk,' she said firmly.

'Of course. But we need other things also,' he said, and tossed in packets of parma ham and diced pancetta. He found pasta from his own country, and got into an animated conversation with a woman at the cheese counter before making his selection. 'Now we need the ingredients for *insalata*,' he said, and Laura, very conscious of envious glances, followed in his wake as he made for the fruit and vegetable section.

When they reached the checkout at last Laura grabbed Domenico's wrist. 'I pay for this,' she hissed in his ear.

'No, you do not,' he answered, and gave her a look of blue, limpid innocence. 'It is just a coffee maker and a few trifles of food. Surely you will allow me the pleasure of this?'

Defeated, Laura watched the objects sailing through the checkout, and winced when the total was announced. 'How are we going to carry this lot?' she asked as Domenico pushed the loaded trolley to the entrance.

'It is a doddle!' He smiled in triumph, took out his phone, and rang one of the taxi firms listed near the door. '*Allora*, we wait a little,' he said as they went outside. 'We can plan our menu for dinner. Or would you like to go out tonight?'

But Laura had no intention of letting Domenico spend any

more money that day. 'If you'll be happy with something simple I'd rather eat at home.'

'*Bene*, so would I. But I shall do the cooking. Just a simple tomato sauce for the pasta, a few crisp morsels of pancetta, some Parmigiano, and we have a feast.'

'I wondered why you bought so many tomatoes.' Laura gave him a radiant smile.

'Why do you smile at me so?' he asked in an undertone.

'Because I just love being here with you like this, doing ordinary things. Normally I look on shopping as an unavoidable chore. With you it was something to enjoy.'

'When we are married,' he said, leaning nearer, 'our entire life will be something to enjoy, Laura.'

The time they spent together proved Domenico's point. Laura had suggested the stay in her flat to find out if they could live together in harmony at such close quarters, and the experiment was a success. They talked non-stop, learning everything they could about each other as they lingered over breakfast, went out for a late lunch, but made dinner together at home. They rode on the Docklands Light Railway for Domenico to experience Laura's daily commute to the bank, and went up in the London Eye to marvel at the views. The only shadow on the entire time came on the Sunday evening while they were preparing dinner together. Laura answered the phone and frowned.

'Why, Edward, what a surprise,' she said, very distinctly, and made a face as Domenico smiled wolfishly.

'Just a call to ask how you are. I thought we might go out for a drink.'

'I'm afraid I can't,' she said politely. 'I have a friend staying with me for the weekend.'

'Bring her along too. Or I could come round to you. I can bring a bottle.'

'I'm afraid my friend wouldn't like that, he's not here for long,' said Laura, wishing that Edward could see the domesticity of the scene. One of Domenico's sauces bubbled on the stove, filling the air with savoury fragrance, half-full wineglasses stood on the coffee-table and Sunday papers were scattered on the floor in front of the sofa.

'Oh. I see,' said Edward stiffly.

'Are you settling in well in the new job?' she asked, sucking in her breath as two arms closed round her like steel bands.

'Very well, thanks. You're still in Docklands?'

'I certainly am. Work as usual tomorrow, unfortunately, so thanks for ringing. Goodnight.'

The moment she put the phone down Domenico turned her in his arms. 'I am a *friend* of yours?' he demanded. 'Why did you not tell him I am your lover?'

'It's nothing to do with him!'

'Did he sleep in your bed?' said Domenico through his teeth.

Laura's eyes flashed angrily. 'No, he did not! Edward and I were just friends.'

'But he wanted to be your lover. It is my turn to feel jealous.' Domenico released her, but only to turn out the heat under the sauce before picking her up to carry her to the bedroom, a gleam in his eye. 'He still wants you, this doctor of yours. But you are *mine*.'

If she'd had any doubt on the point beforehand, the following interlude convinced Laura beyond all possible doubt. As a lover Domenico was normally tender as well as passionate. But this time, fuelled by jealousy, he took possession of her like a conqueror, setting every part of her on fire as he took her to the very brink again and again until he felt her fingernails digging into his shoulders as she gasped in the throes of climax, and with a shout of triumph he surrendered to his own release and collapsed on her, his face buried against her breasts.

Heart hammering against his damp face, Laura smoothed

a hand over his ruffled dark hair, a smile playing at the corners of her mouth. Making love was the only activity that ever left Domenico dishevelled.

'Are you better now?' she enquired when she had breath to speak, and he raised his head to look at her.

'Much better. I was jealous.'

'I know.'

'Are you hungry?'

Laura thought about it. 'Yes. But I don't think I can move quite yet.'

'I am crushing you.' He rolled over and drew her with him, frowning as he smoothed the hair back from her face. 'That has not happened before.'

'What, exactly?'

'The urge to make every part of you know it belonged to me.'

'Believe me, Domenico, every little part got the message!'

He smiled triumphantly. *'Bene.'*

'Now, I need food, Gian Domenico—a heaping plate of complex carbohydrates smothered in whatever you're brewing up in that pan out there.'

He laughed and kissed her at length, then rolled out of bed and stood up, stretching his nude, graceful body before he spun round, seized her hand and pulled her with him into the bathroom. 'Before we eat we shower, yes?'

'You bet. Hand over that frilly cap thing, please.' Laura made a face at him. 'If I have to dry this hair before I eat I won't be answerable for the consequences.'

'Use shorter words, *per favore*,' he ordered. 'Making love to you is good in every other way, but bad for my English vocabulary.'

Laura grinned as she stuffed her hair into the cap. 'You mean I fried your brains.'

For answer Domenico deposited her in the shower and

turned on the cold water, avoiding her flailing arms as he joined her.

'Beast,' she gasped, turning the switch to warm.

'I would enjoy making you warm again,' he said, nuzzling her neck.

'Not before I eat!'

Later, after they'd consumed bowls of pasta with a sauce of tomatoes simmered with garlic, red onion and chillies, Domenico drew Laura down with him on the sofa and fed her grapes, one by one.

'How decadent,' she murmured drowsily. 'Like a Roman orgy.'

'I am Venetian, not Roman,' he reminded her. 'How do you feel now, Laura?'

'Well fed and well loved!'

'*Bene.* I feel this, too.' He smiled quizzically. 'But it is not what I mean. We have been together almost every minute since we left the hotel. Is that long enough to show you that we can be happy living together always?'

So Domenico had been aware of her experiment all along. 'I need longer than that!'

He sighed deeply. 'So do I, but I must return to Venice on Tuesday morning.'

'And I have to go to work tomorrow.'

'If you must get up early we should go to bed. But only to sleep. You look tired, *amore*.'

'No wonder! Your reaction to Edward's phone call was exhausting.'

'How did he know you had been injured?'

'He saw me at the hospital. I didn't know Edward had transferred there.'

'So he works in the neighbourhood!'

'And works very long hours, like all hospital doctors,' said Laura firmly.

Domenico looked down his nose. 'If he rings you again,

tell him the truth, *per favore*. He must be convinced that there is no hope for him.'

'There never was any hope for him in that way.'

'I could make it even clearer,' said Domenico silkily, 'if you give me the name of this hospital.'

'Certainly not. Now, weren't you saying something about bed?'

He gave her a narrowed look. 'You think you will seduce me into forgetting about this Edward, yes?'

Laura smiled slowly. 'Oh, yes.'

He caught her close. 'You are right.'

Next morning Laura had to wrench herself out of Domenico's arms to get up. Hating the thought of leaving him for the best part of the day, she shut herself into the bathroom to let him sleep, but when she came out in her dressing gown, face and hair ready for the day, the scent of coffee was in the air and Domenico was leaning against the window ledge fully dressed, waiting to watch as she put her clothes on.

'*Buon giorno,*' he said, and kissed her on both cheeks. 'When you are ready I will give you coffee.'

'Why,' said Laura as she slid out of her dressing gown, 'do you like to watch me dress? From a male point of view I would have thought the reverse process more interesting.'

'I like that, too. Very much. But to watch you cover your delicious body with those prim clothes you wear to work—' He threw out his hands. 'I cannot explain.'

'I've certainly never had an audience for it before!'

Domenico smiled smugly. 'This is just for me, yes?'

'Just for you,' she agreed. 'But only because you make such great coffee,' she added as he handed her a cup.

'I will miss you so much today,' he said, sighing. 'Would you like to go out to dinner tonight, *tesoro*?'

Laura shook her head. 'I want every moment here alone with you, not in some restaurant with other people.'

'Ah, Laura, *ti amo*!' Domenico relieved her of the coffee-cup and took her in his arms. 'Tell me you love me.'

'Surely you know I do by now?' She smiled. 'If not I'll try to convince you when I come home.'

'I will look forward to this all day.' He kissed her cheek very carefully.

Laura handed him her spare key. 'You'd better have this in case you want to go out. See you tonight.' She reached up to give Domenico a swift kiss and forced herself to leave him.

Laura made sure she arrived home early for once. She unlocked the door, expecting a warm welcome, but to her disappointment there was no one in the flat. Then she smiled as she saw the note anchored down by the kettle.

Amore, I am shopping. I will see you very soon. D.

The doorbell rang while Laura was hanging her jacket in the wardrobe and she rushed through the living room to open the door. Her radiant smile died abruptly. Instead of Domenico it was Edward, with flowers.

'Someone left the building as I arrived so I was able to come straight up.' He handed her the small bouquet.

'Thank you for the flowers, but I'm sorry, I can't ask you in.' Laura stood square in the doorway, keeping him outside on the landing. 'I'm expecting Domenico back any minute.'

'Is this the "friend"? I thought he would have gone by now.' Edward scowled. 'He's your lover, I suppose?'

'Yes, he is,' she said bluntly.

'Is he your reason for turning me down?'

'No. He was nothing to do with it. I met Domenico later, on a trip to Venice.' *Go, go,* ordered Laura silently.

'Love at first sight, I suppose,' he snapped, staring moodily into the stairwell. Then he smiled suddenly. 'By the way,

Laura,' he said, raising his voice, 'I trust there were no complications after losing the baby?'

'No—' Laura stopped dead as Domenico came into view. 'Hi, you're back,' she said inanely. 'Let me introduce you. Domenico Chiesa—Dr Edward Lassiter.'

'Piacere,' said Domenico tersely.

'Hello, there.' Edward acknowledged him with a brief nod, then smiled smugly at Laura. 'Must dash. See you.'

She closed the door on him in relief. 'Sorry about that.'

Domenico eyed her in unsettling silence for a moment. 'Why did he come here tonight?' he demanded.

'To ask if you were my reason for turning him down.'

Domenico gave her a look that rang alarm bells in her head. 'As I came up the stairs I heard him ask a quite different question.'

Laura looked away quickly, powerless to control the rush of colour in her face. 'He was referring to a friend of mine, who lost a baby recently. Edward was on duty when I rushed her to the hospital.'

'What friend is this?' he demanded.

She turned to face him. 'You know I can't tell you her name, Domenico.'

'Why not?'

'It's a private, personal thing. I promised her I wouldn't tell a soul. Ever.'

Domenico flung away to the window, to stare blindly at the lights of London, desperately wanting to believe Laura. But her face had flushed with such obvious guilt it was impossible to ignore the doubts gnawing at him. He took in a deep breath and turned round to look at her, his heart contracting when he saw that the colour had drained from her face, leaving it milk-pale. 'Laura, are you asking me to believe that a busy doctor came here tonight just to ask about your *friend*?' he asked at last.

Her eyes narrowed. 'What exactly are you implying?'

Suddenly his suspicions boiled to the surface. 'I think that you are the one who had this *aborto*! Why in the name of God did you not tell me?'

Laura felt as though every drop of blood in her veins had frozen solid. She stared at his haggard face in icy outrage. 'How can you possibly believe such a thing?' she demanded.

He seized her by the shoulders, his olive skin ashen as his eyes bored down into hers. 'Tell me the truth, Laura! Were you expecting my child?'

'No, I was not.' Her eyes clashed with his angrily. 'Take your hands off me.'

Domenico's hands dropped, but his eyes stayed locked with hers. 'So why did Edward speak of this mysterious other woman? In my country doctors never reveal details of their patients.'

'They don't here, either. Edward was too clever to name names. I suppose he saw you coming up the stairs and seized the moment to settle old scores.' Laura stared back at him, her eyes unwavering.

'How did he know who I was?'

'I mentioned your name and told him I met you in Venice. One look at you was enough to tell him who you were.' She stepped back, her eyes remote and cold as discs of gold glass. 'Edward waited quite a while to get his own back on me for the ring episode, but he did an excellent job when he finally got round to it.'

Domenico felt stabbed by sudden doubt. He threw out a hand. 'Laura, just give me the name of this friend who lost a baby and I will apologise with all my heart.'

'I can't do that. I don't want your apologies, either,' she said scathingly. 'Words are easy. After all, not so long ago you promised to love me forever, and like a fool I believed you meant it.'

'I did mean it!' He made an involuntary move towards

her, his mouth twisting as she backed away. 'It is the truth, Laura.'

'Why should I believe you? You refuse to believe me.' She felt suddenly bone-tired. 'Please leave, Domenico. Now. I'm sure your hotel will find a bed for you.'

He stared at her incredulously. 'You mean this?'

'Never more serious in my life,' she assured him, with indifference that so obviously enraged Domenico she felt a fleeting surge of triumph.

For a moment or two the silence throbbed like a living presence in the room as they stood motionless, staring into each other's eyes.

'Be very careful. If I go now, Laura,' he warned at last, his voice utterly devoid of emotion, 'I will not come back.'

She shrugged. 'Fine by me. I'll ring for a taxi.'

'Do not trouble. I shall do that myself,' he said with hauteur, and strode into the bedroom.

Laura stared after him in misery, feeling as though her world were breaking in pieces around her. But after a moment she squared her shoulders and turned away to find a vase for the flowers Edward had picked up at a garage, from the tag on the wrapping paper. Shaken and sick, she fiddled with them blindly until Domenico returned with his luggage.

'The taxi will be here in five minutes,' he informed her curtly. 'If you wish I can go outside to wait for it.'

She shrugged. 'It's raining. You'd better wait in here.'

'You can endure my presence that long?' he said with biting sarcasm, flinging the bags down.

'Actually, no, I can't.' She threw the flowers in the wastebin and rounded on him like an angry tigress. 'You wait here. I'll take the bedroom. Goodbye.'

But as she made for the bedroom door Domenico startled her by seizing her in his arms. He glared down into her outraged eyes for a moment, then crushed his mouth to hers.

'*Arrivederci*,' he snarled, and put her away from him. He picked up the bags, threw open the door, then strode through it and slammed it shut behind him.

CHAPTER ELEVEN

NONE of the staff at the Forli Palace, not even those who remembered the disaster of his cancelled wedding years before, had ever seen Gian Domenico Chiesa in the mood that enveloped him like a dark miasma on his return from London. He was perfectly courteous, always approachable, and worked longer hours than anyone, but the blue eyes so much admired by female staff members were curiously lifeless, as though a light had been snuffed out behind them.

Domenico knew that he was causing comment among his staff, but could not summon the energy to care. And he spent so little time at his apartment after the London trip that he seriously began to consider selling it. He no longer felt pleasure in his retreat. He saw Laura everywhere: on the balcony, hanging over the rail to look at the water traffic, or in his sitting room, asleep beside him on the sofa, or, most vivid of all, in his arms in his bed. When he walked through the Piazza San Marco he sometimes caught sight of a woman with long fair hair and felt such an intense longing to speak to Laura it was almost pain. But too proud to risk rejection, he never actually rang her. And he gave up all idea of doing so when the mobile phone he'd given her arrived at the Forli Palace. There was no note—nor, he thought bitterly, had he expected one.

He took to work as an antidote, but however many hours he put in it was impossible to put Laura from his mind. Domenico knew that his parents were worried, but he made excuses to avoid visits to the beautiful farmhouse they were restoring in Umbria. He was in no mood to answer his mother's probing questions. Lack of sleep became so much

153

part of his life that on a trip to Florence for a meeting with the board of the Forli Group comments were made about his health by Lorenzo and Roberto Forli. He brushed them aside, used long hours as explanation, and politely refused Roberto's offer to take over for him any time he felt like a break. Getting away was useless. The pain would merely travel with him. He knew that he would forget the anguish of his parting with Laura one day. Of course he would. But one day seemed a long way off.

Just like Domenico, Laura buried herself in work, and no longer took any pleasure in her flat. It was an effort to return to it every night. Her bright idea of bringing Domenico home to it for his stay had backfired on her. His presence haunted the place. No matter how often she washed the sheets the scent of him seemed to linger in her bed. She sent the mobile phone back to him as soon as she bought a new one, and only the cost of postage to Venice decided her against doing the same with the coffee maker.

In her determination to forget Domenico, she made two drastic changes to her life. She bought a car and had her hair cut.

When Laura drew up outside Briar Cottage one Saturday afternoon Isabel came hurrying to see the new purchase, then stared in amazement as her daughter got out of the car.

'Good heavens!'

'Same old me—new hair,' said Laura blithely. 'I had it done this morning, which is why I couldn't make it last night, as usual. What do you think of the little car?'

'Looks good. Where did you get it?'

'Claire's boyfriend went with me to buy it. According to Ben, a good-looking blonde gets taken for a ride if she buys a car on her own,' said Laura, rolling her eyes.

Isabel laughed and kissed her, then stood back to admire the new haircut. In the late afternoon sun the hair gleamed like burnished gold. A longish fringe swept to one side of Laura's forehead and the rest curved under slightly just short of her shoulders.

'Please say you like it, Mother.' Laura smiled brightly. 'It's a lot easier to cope with like this in the mornings.'

'Which follow a lot of late nights, by the circles under your eyes,' observed her mother. 'But I love the hair. Now, bring your bag and have some tea to see you through to supper. You've lost weight.'

Laura did as she was told but refused the cake offered with tea. 'Sorry—big lunch. How's Abby?'

'Enjoying life, thank God. She's made friends—both sexes—and revels in the work, which is no surprise.' Isabel sighed. 'Otherwise she behaves as though nothing happened. Maybe that's a good thing. I wish I could be sure.'

Laura smiled bleakly. 'Your daughters don't have much luck with men, do they?'

'Abby seems to be coping rather better than you right now.' Isabel paused for a moment. 'Laura, I haven't asked what went wrong between you and Domenico, but I can't help feeling worried. One minute you were on cloud nine, then wham! You were down in the depths.'

Because six long weeks had crawled by since the night Domenico walked out of the flat, Laura decided it was time to put her mother in the picture.

'It was Edward's fault,' she said baldly.

'Edward?' said Isabel, taken aback.

'He came to the flat when Domenico was there.' Laura gave a terse description of the episode.

Isabel's face blanched when she heard about Edward's parting shot. 'He knows about *Abby*?'

'Afraid so. It was just bad luck that he was on duty when I took her in.'

'No need to tell me what happened next, then. Domenico thought Edward meant you?'

'Of course he did. Edward finally got his revenge. I told Domenico that Edward was asking after a friend of mine, but he didn't believe a word of it because I wouldn't give him a name.' Laura smiled bitterly. 'Domenico was convinced I was the guilty party so I told him to pack his bags and leave.'

'For heaven's sake, Laura, you should have explained,' said Isabel, appalled.

'How could I? I promised Abby I wouldn't tell a soul.'

'She wouldn't have minded in this instance!'

'Mother, I promised her.' Laura's chin lifted. 'Besides, that's not the point. Domenico should have believed me.'

'When you lied to him did you blush as usual?'

Laura looked mutinous. 'Of course I did. I probably looked the picture of guilt. But that's irrelevant. He should have trusted me.' Her eyes hardened. 'Especially as up until that point he was all for getting married in the New Year.'

Isabel blinked. 'Goodness! That was sudden.'

'I agree. So, practical to the last, I insisted we got to know each other better first.' Laura's eyes flashed gold fire. 'How right I was.'

'I suppose so, but I can't help feeling sorry. I like Domenico. Far more than I ever did Edward.' Isabel looked thoughtful. 'Though it amazes me that he abandoned medical ethics out of petty revenge. His parents would have a fit.'

'Since you're unlikely to discuss it with them at your bridge club they'll never know, hopefully.' Laura heaved a sigh. 'But Edward's punchline convinced Domenico it was me. In Italy, he informed me, doctors never discuss other patients.'

Isabel raked a hand through her hair, frowning. 'It infuriates me to think that Edward used Abby to ruin your life. Can't you report him to the British Medical Council, or something?'

'Believe me, I thought of it. But he didn't name names, Mother, so it probably wouldn't wash. But don't worry, I sorted it. I asked Edward to meet me at a café and told him I'd go to his superiors if he ever mentioned Abby again.' Laura's eyes gleamed coldly. 'He got the message, believe me.'

'That's my girl!' Isabel got up to clear away. 'Have you heard from Domenico since?'

'No. I sent the phone he gave me to the Forli Palace, and I've changed the number in the flat, remember? So even if he wanted to contact me he couldn't.' Laura smiled valiantly. 'End of story.'

But in her heart of hearts Laura had hoped that Domenico would write to apologise, or at least to acknowledge receipt of the mobile phone. He had not. And she pined. And bitterly regretted having her hair cut as an act of defiance Domenico wouldn't even know about. Wild horses wouldn't have made her admit it, but she'd wanted to cry her eyes out after the hairdresser had finished with her. And the general reaction on the trading floor at the bank on Monday made her regret it even more. Her reception couldn't have been more rowdy if she'd appeared in a black satin basque and fishnets. Laura parried all the comments with her usual Ice Maiden smile, and let off steam by swimming several lengths of the pool that night, followed by a thorough workout in the gym. She felt tired enough afterwards to enjoy a peaceful supper in front of the television, and got up to answer the telephone without her usual leap of hope that it might, just might, be Domenico.

'Hi,' said Fen. 'How's things, Miss Green?'

'OK, Mrs Tregenna. How's married life?'

'Just as blissful as living in sin. Only now I'm wearing a wedding ring for the sin part.'

'Thank you for sharing that, Fen!'

'Talking of weddings, we received a belated but absolutely

wonderful present today,' continued the bride. 'Guess what it is?'

'Surprise me.'

'It's the most fabulous chandelier with gold threads twined in the glass. From Murano,' added Fen significantly. 'Perfect for our dining room because it just happens to match the candlesticks you bought us. Isn't that a strange coincidence?'

'Lots of chandeliers in Murano, Fen.'

'This was specially ordered by Domenico, smarty pants. He was obviously with you when you bought the candlesticks.'

'Yes.'

'Just yes?'

Laura sighed. 'He was kind enough to help me with my shopping. Satisfied?'

'Not really. Incidentally, Jess tells me that Lorenzo and Roberto are a bit concerned about cousin Domenico. He came to a board meeting recently looking terrible. Jess thinks the new woman is no longer in his life. She's obviously dumped him.'

'What a shame.'

'Hey, this is Fen you're talking to, Laura Green. I may have been on a pink cloud the day of my wedding, but I noticed that Gian Domenico hot-footed it down to you when he found you were missing, then came back later with a face like thunder. I'd bet my new wedding ring that you're this mystery woman of his and you had a little tiff. I get your voicemail every time I try to find out, and you text me back instead of having a real chat.'

'Oh, all right,' said Laura, resigned. 'We did fall out, for reasons I won't bore you with.' Actually, she longed quite violently to pour out her unhappiness to Fen as she'd always done, but this time it was impossible without bringing Abby into it. 'I'm sorry that Domenico's off colour,' she said instead. This wasn't true. She was fiercely glad to hear that he was no better than she was. 'You haven't heard the big news, then?' she went on, in an effort to divert Fen.

'What big news?'

'I've bought a car.'

'Wow. At last!'

'And—are you sitting comfortably?—I've cut my hair.'

Isabel Green was taking advantage of half-term for a short holiday with her friend Janet, which meant that Laura had no trip to Stavely to look forward to at the end of the week.

'Do something nice over the weekend, darling,' said Isabel. 'I'll see you the following Friday.'

Laura's plan for the weekend was to keep as busy as possible. Laundry, household chores, shopping, ironing, and then a party Ellie and Claire were giving jointly on Saturday night. Now she had a car there would be no comment when she refused a second glass of wine, and, better still, she could leave whenever she liked, instead of the usual hassle of sharing taxis with people who liked staying on later than she did.

After carrying out her plan for the day, Laura was not in much of a party mood later as she brushed her damp hair into its new shape. She felt even less so when she eyed her full-length reflection in the butterfly-print dress. The effect was different with the new-length hair, too girly by far for her liking, and she felt a sudden urge to strip off the dress—and the memories that went with it—and spend the evening at home with a video. But with a sigh she picked up her bag and collected her car keys. She would turn up at the party, as faithfully promised, and even try to enjoy it in the way she would have once, before her trip to Venice.

Later in the evening a taxi drew up in Bow outside the converted match factory that housed Laura's flat. The passenger paid the driver and pressed the bell marked 'L. Green'. When there was no response he pressed the bell again and stood still for some time, eyeing the keys in his hand. At last he unlocked the main entry door and mounted the familiar stairs to the first floor. He pressed the buzzer on the door of Laura's flat with no hope that she would open it. And even if she did, he thought grimly, she might slam it shut again the moment she saw his face. At last he unlocked the door, opened it a little and called her name. Lights were on inside but there was no answer. He rubbed a hand across his eyes and wished he'd asked the taxi driver to wait.

Domenico had never felt more tired in his life as he went inside and closed the door. A wash, he decided, and shrugged off his jacket. Cold water on his face might help. But to reach the bathroom he must cross Laura's bedroom. With a strong feeling of intrusion he went into her room and stopped dead just inside the door when her familiar perfume sent a wave of such desire roaring through his body he felt dizzy. He stood with eyes closed and hands clenched for a moment or two, then took in a deep breath and went into the bathroom. And instead of desire felt a stab of pain at the sight of the absurd frilly shower cap and the small white robe hanging behind the door.

White-hot jealousy seared him as it struck him that a man might accompany Laura back to the flat, and instead of washing his face he returned to the living room in a sudden desperate hurry to get out of there. But first he must leave a note with her key. He shook his head to clear it, took a diary and his fountain pen from his jacket and sat down on the sofa to compose a note. When his sleep-starved brain refused to translate the words into English he rubbed his eyes in despair. If he could just rest for a while perhaps his mind would work again…

When Laura got back to Bow she manoeuvred the car into her slot in the basement parking area and went up in the empty lift barefoot, dangling her killer heels by the straps.

She padded along the hall from the lift to her door, yawning as she closed it behind her, then clapped a hand to her mouth to stifle a scream when she saw a man sprawled, dead to the world, on her sofa.

CHAPTER TWELVE

LAURA'S heart beat a crazy tattoo as she tiptoed across the room to look down at her visitor. He lay with legs outstretched and head back, utterly motionless, a leather diary and a fountain pen near the hand trailing on the floor. His face looked thinner, she noted with a pang, expecting the black lashes to fly up at any moment. But Gian Domenico Chiesa was dead to the world. *Dead?* In a panic Laura touched a finger to his wrist, but his pulse was steady and slow, and she shied away, embarrassed, wondering how long he'd been here. More importantly *why* he was here, when he'd sworn never to come back. Yet here he was, so he obviously still had her key.

In all fairness she could have changed the locks. And the fact that she hadn't proved that she'd hoped, deep down, that Domenico would come back some day. Well, here he was. So the obvious move was to wake him and demand an explanation. But he looked so unutterably weary lying there she hadn't had the heart to do it. Domenico's sleeping face looked drawn, and showed every minute of his eleven-year seniority over her. She backed away as he said something, but Domenico was talking in his sleep, muttering in fragmented Italian she couldn't understand. She eyed him in alarm as he started threshing about. Any minute now he would land on the floor with a bump. She laid a gentle hand on his wrist, and he started violently, then opened the eyes that still had the power to flip her heart over in her chest.

'Laura?' He staggered to his feet, swaying slightly, and she put out a hand, but dropped it again before it could touch him. *'Mi scusi!'* he said hoarsely. 'I did not mean to sleep.'

'How long have you been here?' she asked coolly.

'I am not sure.' He looked at his watch then swore under his breath, dark colour rising along his cheekbones. '*Dio*, it is long past midnight. I did not intend—again forgive me. Because you were not here I thought only to leave your key with a note.'

'I see,' she said distantly. 'Normally I spend weekends in Stavely, but my mother is away.'

He nodded. 'I know this.'

'Really? How?'

He rubbed a hand over his eyes. 'I will explain. But first I must apologise for intruding.'

'It was certainly a surprise to find you dead to the world on my sofa,' she agreed coldly. 'Particularly since you swore you'd never come back here again.'

'I wanted to see you,' he said, and swallowed dryly. 'It is great audacity to ask, but could you allow me to make some coffee?'

'I'll do it,' Laura said firmly, and set to work in a silence neither of them broke until the fragrant brew was ready. She filled two beakers and handed one to Domenico.

'*Grazie,*' he said gratefully.

'Would you like something to eat?'

He shook his head and downed a gulp of coffee like a man in need of caffeine to survive. Looking slightly better, he eyed her objectively, as though seeing her clearly for the first time. 'You have cut your beautiful hair!'

'I felt like a change. I bought a second-hand car, too.' She smiled sardonically. 'Claire's boyfriend went along to make sure I got a good deal. No chance of this for a dumb blonde on her own, apparently.'

'No one could think of you as such.' His mouth twisted. 'You have changed, Laura.'

'So have you.'

He shrugged. 'But I look years older while you look even younger than before.'

Laura sat in the small basket chair and waved him to the sofa. 'You'd better sit down.' Before you fall down, she added silently.

Domenico did as she said, looking very different from the man she'd first met in Venice. His beautiful shoes were the best thing about him. His jeans and blue shirt had suffered for having been slept in, there were dark rings under his eyes, a growth of stubble darkened his jaw and his thick, waving hair was wildly untidy.

'I apologise for my appearance,' he said ruefully.

'Never mind that. Tell me how you know my mother is away.'

'Mrs Green rang me at the hotel,' he said, startling her.

'How did she know you were in London?'

'Not London. Your mother rang the Forli Palace, Laura.'

'She rang *Venice*?' she said incredulously.

'Yes, but I was not there at the time. She left a message for me, with a telephone number, and I contacted her immediately it was given to me.' He took in a deep breath. 'I thought something had happened to you.'

Laura licked lips that were suddenly dry. 'When was this?'

'Yesterday. Your mother was with your sister in Cambridge. Abigail answered when I rang, and explained that she was the "friend" you took to the hospital. She gave me a very stern lecture for doubting you, but your mother was much kinder.' He looked up at Laura. 'I understand now that you could not reveal Abby's secret.' His eyes darkened. 'I would so much like to meet the *bastardo* who did this to her.'

'Did Abby tell you who it was?'

'No. Her concern was for you, Laura. And her disapproval was for me,' he added wryly.

Laura smiled at the thought of it.

'This pleases you?' he asked.

'I can just see Abby telling you off. But I'm sure my mother made you feel better.'

'She was very honest with me,' said Domenico sombrely. 'She knew I could not ring you, but she thinks I should have written to you.'

Laura shrugged. 'Why should you want to?'

'I did not want to.' His eyes met hers. 'You hurt my heart *and* my pride, Laura.'

'I had good reason!'

'But before I spoke with Abigail I did not know the truth. When I did I thought of writing to you, but I speak English better than I write it. I could not hope to put my feelings into words.' He shot her a wry look. 'Nor could I ask my assistant to write such a letter for me.'

His assistant, thought Laura with a pang. 'You engaged someone, then?'

'My father insisted. My Forli cousins are convinced I am ill from overwork, and talked with my parents. *Allora*, I now have help I do not want.' The bloodshot blue eyes locked with Laura's. 'Hard work is not my problem.'

She looked away. 'If you've spoken to my mother, why didn't you just ring me instead of writing to say—whatever you wanted to say?'

Domenico threw out his hands. 'She would not give me your new phone numbers without your permission, so I decided there was only one thing to do. I took advantage of Roberto's offer of help and was fortunate enough to get a flight here today.'

'You came a long way on the off chance of finding me in on a Saturday night,' she said coolly.

Domenico threw out a hand. 'Since I could not ring, what else could I do? Because you were not here I tried to write a note to leave with your key, but while I tried to translate the words into English I fell asleep. I knew nothing more until you woke me.' He looked at his watch and got up. '*Dio!* I must go to my hotel, and let you sleep.'

Fat chance of that, thought Laura.

Domenico took his phone from his jacket, consulted a card, punched in some numbers and after a brief conversation disconnected and sat down again.

'It is a wait of five minutes,' he informed her. 'Which is good, because it gives me time to say what I have flown from Venice to say.'

'I'm listening.'

'I love you, Laura,' he said simply.

She held her breath, her heart beating thickly as she waited for him to go on, but he sat in silence, his eyes on hers as he waited for her response.

'If you'd told me that before you spoke to my sister I might have believed it,' she said at last, and watched with satisfaction as the colour leached from Domenico's drawn face.

'You will not forgive me,' he said quietly.

'Do you blame me?'

'No.' He threw out his hands in appeal. 'But you looked so guilty when you talked of this friend, Laura. You blushed and would not look at me.'

'Because I'm such a hopeless liar,' she said defensively. 'I had to keep talking about a "friend" instead of my sister.'

His mouth twisted. 'I was so sure it was you that I longed to comfort you, grieve with you. But you sent me away.'

Laura looked him in the eye. 'If I had been expecting your child, Domenico Chiesa, you would have been first to know,' she assured him, and for the first time won a ghost of a smile from him.

'I was angry because you could go through such pain and not tell me, yet confide in your friend the doctor,' he explained.

'I didn't go through anything,' she reminded him. 'I didn't

confide in Edward either. He just happened to be on duty when I took Abby in that day. I was appalled when he referred to it that night. Not because I was afraid you would believe it was me—I never for a moment expected that—but because he was unethical enough to say anything at all.'

The doorbell rang and Domenico got up. 'The taxi is here.'

Laura nodded. 'You'd better go, then.'

Domenico looked at her steadily as he put on his jacket. 'So. Are you going to let this vindictive friend of yours have his victory, Laura?'

She rose to her feet, the chiffon drifting as she moved. 'What do you mean?'

'He wanted to tear us apart—and he succeeded.' He caught her hand. 'If you tell me you no longer love me I will go. And this time I will *not* come back. But you must tell me the truth.' He smiled a little. 'I will know, now, if you lie.'

'I still have feelings for you, yes,' she admitted reluctantly.

'*Bene*. Then I will call for you tomorrow.' Domenico kissed her hand and left without giving her time to consent or refuse.

Laura woke late next morning after the best night's sleep she'd had for a long time. And the moment she opened her eyes she knew the reason why. Domenico was back in her life. The self-assured Domenico Chiesa had changed a lot in the time they'd spent apart, but one look at his sleeping, haggard face had made it clear that she loved him *per sempre*, just as she'd once told him. And he obviously still felt the same or why had he come? They'd given each other pain—six long weeks of it. But now they both had a second chance to make it up to each other she, for one, was going to take full advantage of it.

At ten-thirty her phone rang, and Laura smiled. Domenico hadn't been too tired to make a note of her new number.

'*Buon giorno*, Laura. Did you sleep well?'

'Good morning. I slept very well. Did you?'

'I had more sleep last night than in all the endless time we have been apart.'

'Good. You looked pretty tired last night.'

'I did not look pretty at all last night! Today I look a little better.'

She laughed. 'And how you look is very important to you.'

'Not so much any more. Now I have different priorities. If you will eat lunch with me I will tell you about them, Laura.'

'That would be nice.'

'*Bene*. I shall come for you soon, then.'

What did he mean by soon? Laura rushed through a shower, then brushed damp hair into shape with one hand while she slapped moisturiser on her face with the other. With no time to dither over clothes, she pulled on black cord jeans and a slouchy ice-pink sweater, and because her feet were still protesting after a night spent in four-inch heels slid them into flat suede boots. She was ready and waiting and had just started the coffee maker when the doorbell rang, and with a sigh of relief she ran to snatch off the receiver.

'I am here, Laura,' said Domenico, and she pressed the release button and went out on the landing to watch him come up the stairs. But for once he came up in the lift. When the doors opened she could see why. He was carrying a vast picnic basket in one hand and a cool-box in the other.

'What on earth have you got there?' she said, laughing.

His eyes lit up at the sound as he strode towards her, smiling. 'This is our lunch,' he informed her as she held the door wide for him to pass through.

'You really do look prettier today,' she told him.

Domenico put his burdens down and made her a graceful bow. He wore the same suede jacket, but with dove-grey trousers of impeccable cut and a white wool shirt instead of his signature blue. The circles were less in evidence beneath his eyes, which had lost their bloodshot weariness, but now, by daylight, Laura saw changes that clutched at her heart. His face was leaner, the cheekbones more prominent, and there was even an odd thread of silver in the glossy black hair waving so obediently about his head today. But the smiling self-confidence was back in full force as Domenico kissed her hand, then drew her closer and kissed her on both cheeks.

'You are not pretty, Laura, you are beautiful,' he informed her, surveying her from head to toe.

'I never could get my head round that myself, but since the haircut I feel even less so,' she said with a sigh, and smiled ruefully. 'I could have cried when I saw the result.'

'Then why did you have it cut?'

Laura flushed. 'Guess!'

'To defy me, naturally. I miss that long rope of hair,' he said with regret, 'but you look delightful with shorter hair also. Was this much admired by the *ragazzi* at your bank?'

She pulled a face. 'There was total uproar until they found that only the hair had changed.'

Domenico smiled with satisfaction. 'You are still Ice Maiden?'

'Yes. To them, at least,' she added, her pulse racing at the hot, hungry look he gave her in response. 'Now, explain about the picnic. It's raining out there.'

'It is not raining in here, *carissima*—' He stopped short, then shrugged. 'If you object I will not refer to you so.'

She shook her head. 'I don't object.'

'*Bene,*' he said huskily, and took the basket and box into the small kitchen area. 'I thought we might eat here in private, so that we can talk uninterrupted by waiters, but if you prefer I can take you to lunch at the Ritz.'

'*No*, not the Ritz,' she said quickly. 'It's a wonderful place, but that's where Edward embarrassed me with the ring episode.'

'Ah!' Domenico smiled grimly. 'Then most definitely not the Ritz.'

'You've been clever enough to organise lunch so we'll have our picnic here. But not yet. It's early. I've made coffee.'

He sniffed the air. '*Grazie*. May I take off my jacket? Then I shall put some of this in your refrigerator.' He frowned as he stowed containers away. 'There is very little food in here, Laura. It is a good thing I am here to see you eat properly.'

'A very good thing,' she agreed.

Domenico transferred the last container, closed the fridge, and leaned across the counter to look into her eyes. 'You mean this, Laura?'

'With all my heart,' she said quietly.

He took in a deep breath, but instead of seizing her in his arms, as Laura wanted him to, Domenico filled two mugs with coffee, added a little milk to one and took them across to the small table in front of the sofa. 'Today we shall share the sofa, yes?'

'Yes, Domenico.'

'That is so much what I like to hear.' He drew her down beside him. 'I have things to say. If you say, "Yes, Domenico" in answer to all it will make me very happy.'

She took a fortifying sip of coffee. 'Can I say something first, please?'

'Yes, Laura,' he said promptly, and smiled. 'You see? It is easy.'

She shook her head soberly. 'What I'm going to say isn't easy at all.'

His smile died. 'You no longer love me?'

'I've never stopped loving you, even when you suspected me of doing something I never could, ever.' Laura gulped more coffee and put the mug down, turned to face him and took a deep breath. 'Look, Domenico, I appreciate that abortion is the only solution for some women, but it's not for me.'

Domenico looked startled. 'It does not surprise me, Laura, but why are you telling me this?'

She glared at him. 'Because you accused me of *having* an abortion!'

His eyes widened in horror. '*Cosa?* No! I thought only that you had lost our child and could not bear to tell me—' His eyes filled with sudden comprehension. 'Laura, is this why you sent me away that night?'

She nodded vehemently.

'*Dio*, I know now what is meant by the language barrier!' He let out a deep breath. 'In Italian *aborto* can simply mean miscarriage, Laura.'

She stared at him in dismay. 'Is this true?'

'Any dictionary will confirm it. Your lessons in school did not include this word?'

'No, but I wish they had.' She drew in a deep, unsteady breath. 'It would have saved six long weeks of misery. For me, anyway,'

'For me, also,' he said bitterly.

'After what happened to Abby I was ultra-sensitive on the subject.' Laura shivered. 'Even though she was virtually raped, and didn't want the baby, Abby cried her heart out after she lost it, Domenico. Women have a tough time fighting their hormones.'

With a smothered groan he pulled her close, rubbing his cheek over her hair. 'To think that one word tore us apart!'

'We're together now,' she said into his shoulder.

He turned her face up to his and lowered his head until his lips were a breath away from hers. To her frustration they stayed there, just out of contact, and she slid a hand up into his hair and closed the gap. At the first touch their lips crushed together in hunger and Domenico lifted her onto his lap, his arms hard around her as they kissed with a starving desperation fuelled by the long weeks of separation. When the need for oxygen forced them apart at last he leaned his forehead against hers.

'*Ti amo*, Laura,' he said unsteadily. 'I have been in such need of you, just to hold you in my arms like this. Tell me you love me, *tesoro*.'

'Of course I love you.' She blinked fiercely. 'I've been as miserable as sin since you left me.'

'I did not leave you,' he said with passion. 'You sent me away.'

'And all over a misunderstanding,' she whispered, and stroked a hand down his cheek. 'I'll start more Italian lessons right away, so it never happens again.' Laura drew away suddenly, her face hot. 'Or am I taking too much for granted?'

Domenico smiled indulgently. 'How could you do that? We belong together, Laura *mia*.'

'Yes, Domenico.' She smiled demurely and he laughed.

'*Ottimo!* You learn quickly. But I cannot think clearly like this. You must sit beside me while I say the things I am here to say.'

'Yes, Domenico.' She grinned at him and gave him a quick kiss before sliding off his lap to sit beside him. 'There.'

'Before your mother rang me,' he began, taking her hand, 'I had decided to put my apartment up for sale.'

'*What?*' Laura gazed at him in horror. 'You can't do that!'

Domenico shrugged. 'Without you I could no longer bear to live there.'

'Then I'd better come and live there with you—eventually,' she added hastily as his eyes lit up.

'Soon, Laura,' he said imperiously, 'not eventually. We have wasted enough time apart.' He raised her hand to his lips. 'I came here today with such good intentions, *amore*. I meant to be patient, to court you and show how much I care for you, but I cannot wait. I need your answer now. Say you will marry me.'

'Yes, Domenico.'

'Soon?'

'Yes, Domenico.'

He let out a deep, unsteady breath and drew her back onto his lap, his cheek against her hair as he held her in an embrace that threatened her ribs. 'I love you, Laura,' he said, after a while, in a voice so deep and ragged with emotion it brought tears to her eyes.

'I love you, too,' she said, sniffing, and Domenico tipped her face up to his.

'You are crying!'

'Happy tears!'

He kissed them away, kissed her mouth briefly, and got up. *'Allora,'* he said, clearing his throat. 'Have you had breakfast?'

'No. Have you?'

'No. When I woke up my first thought was you, also the second and third thought, but then I told myself to be practical and ordered a picnic lunch to bring to you.' Domenico smiled at her. 'Food has not been of interest to me lately, but now I am hungry.'

'So am I,' said Laura, and for the first time in weeks found she was starving. 'I could eat a horse.'

He grinned. *'Che peccato!* I did not think to order horse.'

They got out plates, sliced bread and opened containers together, and with much laughter got in each other's way in the confined space before they actually sat together to wolf down slices of Bayonne ham and Norfolk turkey with some of the salad greens Laura had already, along with most of a *ciabatta* loaf, and a glass of the Prosecco Domenico produced from the cool-box.

'That was just lovely,' said Laura with a sigh when their plates were empty.

'I chose well, then?' asked Domenico.

'Very well.' She smiled at him. 'But, gorgeous though it was, the food didn't matter. It was eating it together that made it a feast.'

'*E verita, carissima!*' He kissed her, and went on kissing her with mounting purpose, but with superhuman effort Laura broke away and stood up.

'This place is so small it looks like a slum when it's untidy, so let's clear up before—'

'Before?' whispered Domenico, kissing a flushed ear.

'Before any more talking,' she said severely.

When the kitchen was immaculate, Domenico drew Laura down beside him on the sofa and put his arm round her. '*Amore*, do you remember that I was out shopping that last night when you arrived home?'

'Of course I do. I remember every detail of that night,' she said with a shiver. 'I assumed you'd gone out for wine.'

'Not for wine.' He took a small package from his pocket and handed it to her. 'For this.'

Laura removed wrappings and found a box with a world-famous name on it. She held her breath as she pressed the button and stared in wide-eyed silence as the lid flew open to show a gold ring set with a sparkling stone the colour of expensive cognac.

'I was right,' he said huskily. He took the ring from the box and held it up beside her face. 'It is not as beautiful as your eyes, but it is almost the same colour.'

Laura swallowed hard on the lump in her throat. 'It's breathtaking. Perfect. I've never seen a topaz cut like that.'

Domenico slid it onto her finger, his eyes alight with laughter. 'Ah, Laura, how I love you.'

'You're laughing at me,' she accused. 'Shouldn't you be down on one knee?'

'I thought you did not like such romantic gestures.'

'I would from you, Domenico.'

He slid to one knee immediately, and raised her hand to his lips. 'So, will you marry me, Laura?'

'Yes, please.'

'Even though this is not a topaz? I tell you this,' he added apologetically, 'so that you do not describe it so to someone who knows it is not.'

Laura looked down at the glittering stone. 'What is it, then?'

'It is a champagne diamond, *tesoro*.'

She stared at him speechlessly, then down at the ring, and burst into tears.

'Carissima!' Domenico leapt to his feet and snatched her into his arms. 'If you do not like it I shall buy you another—'

'No!' She hugged him hard, then held her wet face up to be kissed. 'It's beautiful and I love it. But if you'd given me a topaz I would have loved that, too.'

'Ah, Laura.' He drew her down on his lap on the sofa and held her close, kissing away her tears. 'So, *fidanzata mia*, how soon can we be married?'

'We'll need to talk to my mother about that. I'll go to work tomorrow, but take the rest of the week off, so we can go down and see her,' said Laura with decision. 'But for the moment why not ring for a cab and go back to the hotel with the picnic things? You can collect your luggage and check out at the same time.'

Domenico cupped her face in his hands. 'Are you sure of this? I can go back to the hotel each night if you prefer.'

Laura stared at him in astonishment. 'And waste all that money on hotel bills and taxis? Are you mad?'

He laughed. 'My practical Laura!'

'That's me. Practical—*and* yours,' she assured him, and received a passionate kiss in response.

While Domenico was out Laura changed the bed and tidied up the flat, a process that took longer than usual due to frequent pauses to admire her ring. When Isabel Green rang as promised, to report on her return home, her euphoric daughter gave her the glad news.

'You sneaky, wonderful mother to ring Venice. I love you to bits. Do I ever tell you that?'

'Not often,' said Isabel, sounding suspiciously husky. 'But it's nice to know. So all is well?'

'Oh, yes. Very well indeed.' Laura gave a deep sigh of pure contentment. 'I thought we'd take a trip down to Stavely on Tuesday for some wedding talk and stay for a night.'

'Darling, how lovely. I thought Domenico might not be able to spare the time.'

'He doesn't go back until Friday. Oh, and Mother, don't bother making up Abby's bed. Domenico will share mine.'

When Domenico had returned from his round trip Laura threw open the door to him and he put his bags on the floor and took her in his arms, kissing her as though they'd been parted for days.

'I did not mean to be so long,' said Domenico, releasing her. 'Have you missed me?'

Laura grinned as she closed the door. 'Actually, I haven't missed you at all. I've been too busy. I've spoken with Mother, and rung Abby and Fen with the news, and I've got everything ready for supper, and,' she added with emphasis, 'I've put clean sheets on the bed.'

Domenico took in a deep breath. 'Only a few short days ago I believed I would never share your bed again.'

Laura leaned up to kiss him. 'You're not only invited to share mine here, but the one in Briar Cottage, too. I told Mother we'd go down to Stavely on Tuesday.'

Domenico leaned against the counter, watching her with such pleasure Laura took a long time to make supper due to a need to be kissed a lot. While they ate ham omelettes they discussed the best way to please everyone with their wedding plans.

'But if I am truthful it is only you I wish to please,' said Domenico, toasting Laura with the last of the Prosecco.

'If you could please your own family at the same time it would start things off on the right foot,' she pointed out.

He grinned. 'What is this right foot?'

'You know perfectly well! We'll ask Mother,' added Laura. 'She'll know what to do.'

'However we arrange it I shall pay,' said Domenico, and held up a hand at her frown. 'Your mother is a widow and I will soon be her son-in-law. It is only right that I take care of her.'

'That's very sweet of you, darling. We'll talk it over with her and ask her advice. She likes you a lot,' Laura told him. 'Otherwise she wouldn't have rung you in Venice.'

'I am very glad of this,' he said soberly. 'I shall always be grateful to her. Also to Abby for trusting her secret to me. But it disturbs me that this doctor of yours also shares it.'

'It disturbed me, too, so I did something about it.' Laura's eyes glittered as brightly as her ring as she told him about her warning to Edward.

Domenico frowned blackly. 'Did you tell him what grief he had caused us?'

'No fear. I wouldn't give him the satisfaction.' She grinned. 'It was very hot in the café so my blush went unnoticed when I told Edward that you and I were still lovers.'

'It was not a lie.' He leaned to kiss her cheek. 'We shall be lovers *per sempre*.'

Laura turned her mouth up to his for a moment in appreciation. 'Now, let's forget about Edward. I have a practical suggestion to make.'

He smiled indulgently. 'Will I like it?'

'Yes. Let's wash these plates and go to bed.'

Domenico let out a deep breath and kissed her nose. 'I

have been waiting to hear you say this since you mentioned the sheets on your bed—'

'But you wanted me to suggest it first?' she said, grinning at him. 'Do I have to ask now, then?'

'This time only. Never again,' he assured her.

When they were in bed together at last, Domenico took Laura into his arms with such a heartfelt sigh she hugged him hard.

'I have wanted this so much,' he said huskily. 'Not just to make love. Of course I want this very much also—what man would not—but I need to hold you for a long time until I know I am not dreaming.'

'How long?' said Laura, wriggling closer.

He breathed in sharply. 'Not so very long,' he said with difficulty, then stared in surprise as she sat up and turned on her lamp.

'I've got a little present for you.' She opened the drawer in her bedside table and took out a fold of tissue paper.

Domenico sat up to take it from her, his eyes questioning.

'I was given this by my grandmother when I was ten,' she told him. 'I thought you might like it.'

He removed the paper from a small gold locket engraved with the initial 'L' in the cartouche.

'Open it,' said Laura.

Domenico ran his thumbnail along the catch, and gazed in delight at the strand of bright gold hair coiled inside the locket.

'I kept it so you can remember when I'm old and grey,' she said with a catch in her voice.

He closed the locket, clasped the chain round his neck and took her in his arms. '*Mille grazie, innamorata.* I shall treasure this always, and take much pride in showing it to our grandchildren.'

'Do I get a kiss in return?'

'Many kisses!'

Domenico kissed her with hunger, exulting in Laura's response as she caressed his shoulders with urgent hands, her breathing ragged as his kisses moved down her throat to her breasts and the nipples that sprang erect in response to his lips and grazing teeth. She gasped his name as he slid his fingers up her thighs to find the little bud throbbing between them, his caresses taking her to the point of frenzy before he moved to lie between her parted thighs, his arousal erect and ready.

'*Ti amo*, Laura,' he said, in a tone she'd never heard before.

'Then love me now,' she whispered, and with a victorious smile he entered her with a sure, slow thrust that held them transfixed by pure sensation for an instant before they began to move in gradually increasing urgency to achieve, at last, the ultimate, heart-stopping moment of glory.

On a bright December afternoon two months later Laura clutched Domenico's hand as she looked down from the plane at the sunlit canals and gleaming buildings of Venice rising up to meet them.

He leaned nearer. 'You are nervous as the plane lands, *carissima*?'

'No, just excited.' She gave him a dazzling smile. 'Happy, too, Domenico. It was such a lovely day yesterday. Your mother and father were very kind. They seemed to like me.'

He laughed indulgently. 'How could they not? They have always wanted a daughter. They were also much charmed with your mother and sister. Isabel has promised to show them round the countryside at Stavely during their stay.'

'It's very good of them to move out of their place in Umbria for us to honeymoon there.'

'I hope it will not be too cold for you at this time of the year.'

'A Brit like me?' Laura laughed, and shook her head.

Domenico smiled. 'If you are cold I shall think of ways to make you warm again. Do not forget your wrap. You will need it on the water.'

When they left the plane the captain and the flight staff were waiting to see them off, and to Laura's surprise she was presented with a small bouquet of rosebuds along with their congratulations.

'How lovely,' she said to Domenico as they entered the terminal.

'I let them into the secret when I reserved the flight,' he said, smiling smugly.

Laura laughed at him, so happy she wanted to crystallise each second of this day and treasure it. A heavy gold band accompanied the champagne diamond on her finger, she looked her best in a swathe of caramel wool draped over the shoulders of a white wool coat cut by one of Domenico's countrymen, and, best and most important by far, her handsome bridegroom was holding her arm with openly possessive pride. As they entered the airport building a young man came hurrying towards them, smiling, and greeted them in a flood of Italian Domenico stemmed with a raised hand.

'*Basta!* My wife is not fluent in our language yet, Carlo. Speak English.'

'*Mi scusi,*' he said, with a bow to Laura. 'Welcome, Signora Chiesa. Please accept my good wishes.'

'Thank you,' she said warmly, and eyed him closely. 'I think we've met before.'

'This is Carlo Mancini, one of my receptionists at the Forli Palace,' said Domenico. 'But today he will wait for our luggage and deliver it to the apartment before we arrive there. Is everything arranged, Carlo?'

The young man nodded, smiling, and gestured towards the landing stage. 'It awaits, *signore.*'

Laura's eyes widened as Domenico took her hand to lead her through the crowds to the quayside, not to a water taxi as she'd expected, but to a gondola decked with flowers. The smiling *gondoliere* touched his straw hat as Domenico helped her aboard, and Laura gave him a delighted smile and sat down, noting that they were the focus of quite a few tourist cameras when Domenico put his arm round her.

'So this was why we had to make the early flight today,' she said in his ear as the gondolier sank his oar into the water.

Domenico grinned at her, the light in his luminous blue eyes triumphant. 'Enjoy it while you may, Signora Chiesa. We Venetians ride by gondola on our wedding day only. I know my practical bride scorns romantic gestures, but this is tradition, Laura *mia*, even if it is a day late.'

'I love it,' she sighed, watching the late winter sun rippling on the water as the gondolier threaded skilfully through the Grand Canal traffic. She gave him a sidelong look. 'It obviously depends on the gesture and who makes it.'

'From this day these will be made by your husband only,' he warned her.

'Absolutely,' she assured him. 'So tell me again what happens next.'

'We go to the apartment, where Carlo will have delivered our luggage. You can drink some of your favourite tea,' he went on, his arm tightening. 'Later we go to the Forli Palace to meet the staff and eat a celebration dinner. This will be served early so that we can go to bed in good time to prepare for the trip to Umbria tomorrow.'

'Domenico,' she whispered in his ear, 'I notice that bed is featured in the itinerary.'

'But of course.' He grinned at her. 'Brides must expect this.'

The slow, languorous journey down the Grand Canal was the crowning touch to two days Laura would remember all her life, starting with the wedding ceremony in Pennington. Guido and Anna Chiesa had looked on with love as their son slid the wedding ring on his bride's finger, and there'd been some suspicious sniffing in the congregation—not from Isabel Green, as one might have expected, but from Fen, as she'd watched her father escort Laura down the aisle.

Domenico had even persuaded Laura to wear a conventional bridal gown instead of her practical idea of the unworn bridesmaid dress made for Fen's wedding.

'Humour me, *carissima*,' he'd asked, and, because Laura found it hard to say no to anything he wanted she'd given in. Her mother had agreed fervently with Domenico. But Isabel had refused to let him pay.

'I've let you have your way about the reception at the Chesterton, but I must buy my daughter's dress,' she'd said gently, and Domenico had kissed her hand in laughing defeat.

Laura had given in about the dress, but instead of conventional white had chosen a long Chantilly lace sheath the colour of champagne, with a short sleeveless version for Abby. The contrast of the sisters, one so fair and the other so dark, had drawn much admiration from the guests who'd flown from Italy for the wedding, and at the reception afterwards Domenico had made a graceful speech of thanks to Isabel Green for allowing him to marry her beautiful daughter, and welcomed her to Venice with Abby as often as she wished to visit.

'You are dreaming,' said Domenico as Laura gazed at the sunlight gilding the ancient buildings lining the Grand Canal.

'I was thinking of our wedding.' She turned to smile at him. 'You made a great speech.'

'I meant every word. I am very fond of my new mother-in-law, and I think Abby feels warmer towards me now. She is a very lovely girl, Laura. I will take great care of her when she visits us.'

'Are you influenced by what happened to her?'

'Of course. No man must ever hurt her again.'

'I love you so much, Domenico,' said Laura, moving closer. 'I still can't believe we're actually married.'

He laughed, and kissed her cheek. 'When we get home I shall take very great pleasure in removing any doubts, *tesoro*.'

She smiled demurely. 'You removed one or two last night.'

His hand tightened on hers. 'I would have continued to do so this morning, but I had ordered breakfast very early to allow us to reach Heathrow in good time for our flight.'

'I didn't want to get up!'

'I know this.' Domenico chuckled. 'You growled at me like a little tigress when I tried to wake you.'

The sun was setting in a red ball over the Salute as the gondola halted in the narrow canal near the apartment. Domenico gave the *gondoliere* a sizeable tip and to the accompaniment of fervent good wishes helped his bride onto dry land.

'*Allora*, Signora Chiesa, we are here.'

Hand in hand they mounted the steps to the first floor of the building. Domenico unlocked the door, then picked Laura up in his arms to carry her across the threshold. As he set her on her feet she reached up to give him a kiss, then went through the apartment on a tour of inspection, exclaiming over the fresh flowers everywhere before she went out onto the balcony to watch the sun sink into the lagoon. Domenico came behind her to slide his arms round her waist.

'Welcome back to Venice, *tesoro*.'

Laura turned in his embrace, gazing up at him with such love his breath caught in his chest. 'I'm not dreaming, am I?'

He shook his head lovingly. 'No, *sposa mia*, you are not dreaming. You are here, in Venice, in my home and in my heart.'

Their lips met in a long, reverent kiss as though the occasion was too important for mere passion, then they went inside, closing the glass doors on the lagoon night.

'I don't want any tea,' said Laura as they reached the bedroom. 'I want you, Domenico.' She smiled as his eyes darkened and he crushed her close for a moment before undoing her coat.

'We shall celebrate our marriage in the place where we first made love,' he said with satisfaction, and smiled wryly. 'I rarely slept here after you sent me away. You were here with me in the bed, in every room. I could not get you out of my mind.'

'I was the same,' she said huskily. 'Let's make a promise never to quarrel again, Domenico.'

'I do not make promises I cannot keep,' he said regretfully, sliding the zip of her dress down. 'I have a temper; so have you. But I promise we shall never be parted again.'

'When we quarrel we must have make-up love straight away,' she said firmly and stepped out of the caramel jersey dress in the lacy underwear worn for precisely this moment. She slid a suspender from a stocking, but Domenico shook his head and pulled her close to kiss her before scooping her up to lay her on the bed.

'That is my privilege. I will undress you, *tesoro*,' he informed her.

'Will we stop wanting each other so desperately now we are married?' she asked breathlessly.

'Never,' he promised huskily, the process of removing the scraps of lace and satin firing them both to such a state of frenzied arousal that their loving was hot and sweet and utterly satisfying, but very short.

'You are Ice Maiden no longer!' panted Domenico, burying his face against her breasts.

'That gondola ride was to blame—the best foreplay one could ask for,' said Laura breathlessly as she smoothed the damp hair back from her husband's forehead. 'I see now why Venetians keep it for their wedding day!'

Domenico looked up with a grin. 'We shall ride by gondola often if it has that effect on you.'

'The effect on you was just the same!'

'That was nothing to do with the gondola. I will always want to make love to you—every night of our lives.'

'*Every* night?'

'This is a problem?'

'Not for me.' She gave him a cheeky grin. 'After all, I'm a lot younger than you!'

Domenico growled and flipped her on her back, grinning. 'Then before I get too old perhaps I should make love to you again now, yes?'

'That's your male Venetian pride talking again!' She stretched luxuriously and smiled up at him. 'I'm so glad you cancelled the gondola ride that first time, darling.'

'I did so because of your dislike of romantic gestures,' he said, running a possessive finger down her cheek. 'But now I believe that fate prompted me to save the gondola trip for our wedding day. I knew even then, *carissima*, that you were my destiny.'

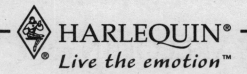

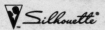
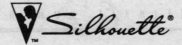

SILHOUETTE Romance®

From first love to forever, these love stories
are fairy tale romances for today's woman.

Modern, passionate reads that are powerful and provocative.

Silhouette® SPECIAL EDITION™

Emotional, compelling stories that capture the intensity
of living, loving and creating a family in today's world.

Silhouette® INTIMATE MOMENTS™

A roller-coaster read that delivers romantic thrills
in a world of suspense, adventure and more.

HARLEQUIN®
INTRIGUE®

WE'LL LEAVE YOU BREATHLESS!

If you've been looking for thrilling tales of
contemporary passion and sensuous love stories
with taut, edge-of-the-seat suspense—then
you'll love Harlequin Intrigue!

Every month, you'll meet six new heroes
who are guaranteed to make your spine tingle
and your pulse pound. With them you'll enter
into the exciting world of Harlequin Intrigue—
where your life is on the line
and so is your heart!

THAT'S INTRIGUE—
ROMANTIC SUSPENSE
AT ITS BEST!

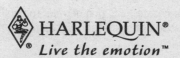

HARLEQUIN®
® *Live the emotion*™